Nora Roberts is the number one *New York Times* bestseller of more than 200 novels. With over 400 million copies of her books in print, she is indisputably one of the most celebrated and popular writers in the world. She has achieved numerous top five bestsellers in the UK, including number one for *Savour the Moment,* and is a *Sunday Times* hardback bestseller writing as J. D. Robb.

Become a fan on Facebook at
www.facebook.com/norarobertsjdrobb
and be the first to hear all the latest from Piatkus
about Nora Roberts and J. D. Robb

www.noraroberts.com
www.nora-roberts.co.uk
www.jd-robb.co.uk

By Nora Roberts

Romantic Suspense

By Nora Roberts

Trilogies and Quartets

The Born In Trilogy:
Born in Fire
Born in Ice
Born in Shame

The Bride Quartet:
Vision in White
Bed of Roses
Savour the Moment
Happy Ever After

The Key Trilogy:
Key of Light
Key of Knowledge
Key of Valour

The Irish Trilogy:
Jewels of the Sun
Tears of the Moon
Heart of the Sea

Three Sisters Island Trilogy:
Dance upon the Air
Heaven and Earth
Face the Fire

The Inn Boonsboro Trilogy:
The Next Always
The Last Boyfriend
The Perfect Hope

The Sign of Seven Trilogy:
Blood Brothers
The Hollow
The Pagan Stone

Chesapeake Bay Quartet:
Sea Swept
Rising Tides
Inner Harbour
Chesapeake Blue

In the Garden Trilogy:
Blue Dahlia
Black Rose
Red Lily

The Circle Trilogy:
Morrigan's Cross
Dance of the Gods
Valley of Silence

The Dream Trilogy:
Daring to Dream
Holding the Dream
Finding the Dream

Nora Roberts also writes the In Death series
using the pseudonym J. D. Robb

Naked in Death
Glory in Death
Immortal in Death
Rapture in Death
Ceremony in Death
Vengeance in Death
Holiday in Death
Conspiracy in Death
Loyalty in Death
Witness in Death
Judgement in Death
Betrayal in Death
Seduction in Death
Reunion in Death
Purity in Death
Portrait in Death
Imitation in Death
Divided in Death

Visions in Death
Survivor in Death
Origin in Death
Memory in Death
Born in Death
Innocent in Death
Creation in Death
Strangers in Death
Salvation in Death
Promises in Death
Kindred in Death
Fantasy in Death
Indulgence in Death
Treachery in Death
New York to Dallas
Celebrity in Death
Delusion in Death

NORA ROBERTS

IN DREAMS &
WINTER ROSE

piatkus

PIATKUS

This edition first published in Great Britain in 2013 by Piatkus

A CIP catalogue record for this book
is available from the British Library.

ISBN 978-0-7499-5852-7

Typeset in Bembo by M Rules
Printed and bound by CPI Group (UK) Ltd, Croydon CR0 4YY

Papers used by Piatkus are from well-managed forests
and other responsible sources.

MIX
Paper from
responsible sources
FSC® C104740

Piatkus
An imprint of
Little, Brown Book Group
100 Victoria Embankment
London EC4Y 0DY

An Hachette UK Company
www.hachette.co.uk

www.piatkus.co.uk

IN DREAMS

Prologue

All he had were the dreams. Without them he was alone, always and ever alone. For the first hundred years of his solitude, he lived on arrogance and temper. He had plenty of both to spare.

For the second, he lived on bitterness. Like one of his own secret brews, it bubbled and churned inside him. But rather than healing, it served as a kind of fuel that pushed him from day to night, from decade to decade.

In the third century, he fell into despair and self-pity. It made him miserable company, even for himself.

His stubbornness was such that it took four hundred years before he began to make a home for himself, to struggle to find some pleasure, some beauty, some satisfaction in his work and his art. Four hundred years before his pride made room for the admission that he may have been, perhaps, just slightly and only partially responsible for what had become of him.

Still, had his actions, his attitude, deserved such a harsh judgment from the Keepers? Did his mistake, if indeed it had been a mistake, merit centuries of imprisonment, with only a single week of each hundred-year mark in which to really live?

When half a millennium had passed, he surrendered to the dreams. No, it was more than surrender. He embraced them, survived on them. Escaped into them when his soul cried out for the simple touch of another being.

For she came to him in dreams, the dark-haired maid with eyes like blue diamonds. In dreams she would run through his forest, sit by his fire, lie willing in his bed. He knew the sound of her voice, the warmth of it. He knew the shape of her, long and slender as a boy. He knew the way the dimple would wink to life at the corner of her mouth when she laughed. And the exact placement of the crescent moon birthmark on her thigh.

He knew all of this, though he had never touched her, never spoken to her, never seen her but through the silky curtain of dreams.

Though it had been a woman who had betrayed him, a woman who was at the root of his endless solitude, he yearned for this dark-haired maid. Yearned for her, as the years passed, as much as he yearned for what had been.

He was drowning in a great, dark sea of alone.

1

It was supposed to be a vacation. It was supposed to be fun, relaxing, enlightening.

It was not supposed to be terrifying.

No, no, terrifying was an exaggeration. Slightly.

A wicked summer storm, a strange road snaking through a dark forest where the trees were like giants cloaked in the armor of mists. Kayleen Brennan of the Boston Brennans wasn't terrified by such things. She was made of sterner stuff. She made a point of reminding herself of that, every ten seconds or so as she fought to keep the rental car on the muddy ditch that had started out as a road.

She was a practical woman, had made the decision to be one quite deliberately and quite clearly when she was twelve. No flights of fancy for Kayleen, no romantic dreams or foolish choices. She had watched – was still watching – such occupations lead her charming, adorable, and baffled mother into trouble.

Financial trouble. Legal trouble. Man trouble.

So Kayleen had become an adult at twelve, and had stayed one.

An adult was not spooked by a bunch of trees and a few streaks of lightning, or by mists that thickened and thinned as if they breathed. A grown woman didn't panic because she'd made a wrong turn. When the road was too narrow, as this one was, to allow her to safely turn around, she simply kept going until she found her way again.

And a sensible person did not start imagining she heard things in the storm.

Like voices.

Should have stayed in Dublin, she told herself grimly as she bumped over a rat. In Dublin with its busy streets and crowded pubs, Ireland had seemed so civilized, so modern, so urbane. But no, she'd just had to see some of the countryside, hadn't she? Just had to rent a car, buy a map, and head out to explore.

But honestly, it had been a perfectly reasonable thing to do. She'd intended to see the country while she was here and perhaps find a few treasures for her family's antique shop back in Boston. She'd intended to wander the roads, to drive to the sea, to visit the pretty little villages, and the great, grand ruins.

Hadn't she booked her stay in a licensed bed-and-breakfast for each night that she'd be traveling? Confirmed reservations ensured there would be no inconvenience and no surprises at the end of each day's journey.

Hadn't she precisely mapped out her route and each point of interest, how long she intended to stay studying each?

She hadn't anticipated getting lost. No one did. The weather report had indicated some rain, but this was Ireland, after all. It had *not* indicated a wild, windy, wicked thunderstorm that shook her little car like a pair of dice in a cup and turned the long, lovely summer twilight into raging dark.

Still, it was all right. It was perfectly all right. She was just a bit behind schedule, and it was partly her own fault. She'd lingered a bit longer than she intended at Powerscourt Demesne on her way south. And a bit longer again at the churchyard she'd come across when she headed west.

7

She was certainly still in County Wicklow, certainly somewhere in Avondale Forest, and the guidebook had stated that the population through the forested land was thin, the villages few and far between.

She had expected to find it charming and atmospheric, a delightful drive on her way to her night's stay in Enniscorthy, a destination she'd been scheduled to reach by seven-thirty. She tipped up her arm, risked a quick glance at her watch, and winced when she saw she was already a full hour late.

Doesn't matter. Surely they wouldn't lock the doors on her. The Irish were known for their hospitality. She intended to put that to the test as soon as she came across a town, a village, or even a single cottage. Once she did, she'd get her bearings again.

But for now . . .

She stopped dead in the road, realizing she hadn't even seen another car for over an hour. Her purse, as ruthlessly organized as her life, sat on the seat beside her. She took out the cell phone she'd rented, turned it on.

And swore softly when the readout told her, as it had since she'd driven into the forest far enough to realize she was lost, that she had no signal.

'Why don't I have a signal?' She nearly rapped the phone

against the steering wheel in frustration. But that would have been foolish. 'What is the point of renting mobile phones to tourists if they're not going to be able to use them?'

She put the phone away, took a deep breath. To calm herself, she closed her eyes, tilted her head back, and allowed herself two minutes of rest.

The rain lashed the windows like whips, the wind continued its feral howl. At jolting intervals the thick darkness was split by yet another lance of blue-edged lightning. But Kayleen sat quietly, her dark hair still tidy in its band, her hands folded in her lap.

Her mouth, full and shapely, gradually relaxed its tight line. When she opened her eyes, blue as the lightning that ripped the sky, they were calm again.

She rolled her shoulders, took one last cleansing breath, then eased the car forward.

As she did, she heard someone – something – whisper her name.

Kayleen.

Instinctively, she glanced to the side, out the rain-spattered window, into the gloom. And there, for an instant, she saw a shadow take shape, the shape of a man. Eyes, green as glass, glittered.

She hit the brakes, jerking forward as the car slid in the mud. Her heart raced, her fingers shook.

Have you dreamed of me? Will you?

Fighting fear, she quickly lowered the window, leaned out into the driving rain. 'Please. Can you help me? I seem to be lost.'

But there was no one there. No one who would – could – have said, so low and sad, *So am I.*

Of course there was no one. With one icy finger she jabbed the button to send the window back up. Just her imagination, just fatigue playing tricks. There was no man standing in the forest in a storm. No man who knew her name.

It was just the sort of foolishness her mother would have dreamed up. The woman lost in the enchanted forest, in a dramatic storm, and the handsome man, most likely a prince under a spell, who rescued her.

Well, Kayleen Brennan could rescue herself, thank you very much. And there were no spellbound princes, only shadows in the rain.

But her heart rapped like a fist against her ribs. With her breath coming fast, she hit the gas again. She would get off of this damned road, and she would get to where she intended to be.

When she got there, she would drink an entire pot of tea

while sitting neck-deep in a hot bath. And all of this . . . inconvenience would be behind her.

She tried to laugh it off, tried to distract herself by mentally composing a letter home to her mother, who would have enjoyed every moment of the experience.

An adventure, she would say. Kayleen! You finally had an adventure!

'Well, I don't want a damn adventure. I want a hot bath. I want a roof over my head and a civilized meal.' She was getting worked up again, and this time she couldn't seem to stop. 'Won't somebody *please* help me get where I'm supposed to be!'

In answer, lightning shot down, a three-pronged pitchfork hurled out of the heavens. The blast of it exploded the dark into blinding light.

As she threw up an arm to shield her eyes, she saw, standing like a king in the center of the road, a huge buck. Its hide was violently white in the slash of her headlights, its rack gleaming silver. And its eyes, cool and gold, met her terrified ones through the rain.

She swerved, stomped on the brakes. The little car fishtailed, seemed to spin in dizzying circles propelled by the swirling fog. She heard a scream – it had to be her own – before the car ran hard into a tree.

And so she dreamed.

Of running through the forest while the rain slapped down like angry fingers. Eyes, it seemed a thousand of them, watched her through the gloom. She fled, stumbling in the muck stirred up by the storm, her bones jolting as she fell.

Her head was full of sound. The roar of the wind, the booming warning of thunder. And under it a thousand voices chanting.

She wept, and didn't know why. It wasn't the fear, but something else, something that wanted to be wrenched out of her heart as a splinter is wrenched from an aching finger. She remembered nothing, neither name nor place – only that she had to find her way. Had to find it before it was too late.

There was the light, the single ball of it glowing in the dark. She ran toward it, her breath tearing out of her lungs, rain streaming from her hair, down her face.

The ground sucked at her shoes. Another fall tore her sweater. She felt the quick burn on her flesh and, favoring her left arm, scrambled up again. Winded, aching, lost, she continued at a limping run.

The light was her focus. If only she could make it to the light, everything would be all right again. Somehow.

A spear of lightning struck close, so close she felt it sear the air, felt it drench the night with the hot sting of ozone. And in its afterglow she saw that the light was a single beam, from a single window in the tower of a castle.

Of course there would be a castle. It seemed not odd at all that there should be a castle with its tower light glowing in the middle of the woods during a raging storm.

Her weeping became laughter, wild as the night, as she stumbled toward it, tramping through rivers of flowers.

She fell against the massive door and with what strength she had left, slapped a fist against it.

The sound was swallowed by the storm.

'Please,' she murmured. 'Oh, please, let me in.'

By the fire, he'd fallen into the twilight-sleep he was allowed, had dreamed in the flames he'd set to blaze – of his dark-haired maid, coming to him. But her eyes had been frightened, and her cheeks pale as ice.

He'd slept through the storm, through the memories that often haunted him even in that drifting place. But when she had come into those dreams, when she had turned those eyes on him, he stirred. And spoke her name.

And jolted awake, that name sliding out of his mind

again. The fire had burned down nearly to embers now. He could have set it roaring again with a thought, but didn't bother.

In any case, it was nearly time. He saw by the pretty crystal clock on the ancient stone mantel – he was amused by such anachronisms – that it was only seconds shy of midnight.

His week would begin at that stroke. For seven days, and seven nights, he would *be*. Not just a shadow in a world of dreams, but flesh, blood, and bone.

He lifted his arms, threw back his head, and waited to become.

The world trembled, and the clock struck midnight.

There was pain. He welcomed it like a lover. Oh, God, to *feel*. Cold burned his skin. Heat scorched it. His throat opened, and there was the blessed bliss of thirst.

He opened his eyes. Colors sprang out at him, clear and true, without that damning mist that separated him for all the other time.

Lowering his hands, he laid one on the back of his chair, felt the soft brush of velvet. He smelled the smoke from the fire, the rain that pounded outside and snuck in through his partially open window.

His senses were battered, so overwhelmed with the rush

of sensations that he nearly swooned. And even that was a towering pleasure.

He laughed, a huge burst of sound that he felt rumble up from his belly. And fisting his hands, he raised them yet again.

'I am.'

Even as he claimed himself, as the walls echoed with his voice, he heard the pounding at the door. Jolted, he lowered his arms, turned toward a sound he'd not heard in five hundred years. Then it was joined by another.

'Please.' And it was his dream who shouted. 'Oh, please, let me in.'

A trick, he thought. Why would he be tortured with tricks now? He wouldn't tolerate it. Not now. Not during his week to be.

He threw out a hand, sent lights blazing. Furious, he strode out of the room, down the corridor, down the circling pie-shaped stairs. They would not be allowed to infringe on his week. It was a breach of the sentence. He would not lose a single hour of the little time he had.

Impatient with the distance, he muttered the magic under his breath. And appeared again in the great hall.

He wrenched open the door. Met the fury of the storm with fury of his own.

And saw her.

He stared, transfixed. He lost his breath, his mind. His heart.

She had come.

She looked at him, a smile trembling on her lips and sending the dimple at the corner of her mouth to winking.

'There you are,' she said.

And fainted at his feet.

2

Shadows and shapes and murmuring voices. They swirled in her head, swelling, fading in a cycle of confusion.

Even when she opened her eyes, they were there. Revolving. What? was her only thought. What is it?

She was cold and wet, and every part of her was a separate ache. An accident. Of course, an accident. But . . .

What is it?

She focused and saw overhead, high overhead, a curved ceiling where plaster faeries danced among ribbons of flowers. Odd, she thought. How odd and lovely. Dazed, she lifted a hand to her brow, felt the damp. Thinking it blood, she let out a gasp, tried to sit up.

Her head spun like a carousel.

'Uh-oh.' Trembling now, she looked at her fingers and saw only clear rainwater.

And, turning her head, saw him.

First came the hard jolt of shock, like a vicious strike to the heart. She could feel panic gathering in her throat and fought to swallow it.

He was staring at her. Rudely, she would think later when fear had made room for annoyance. And there was anger in his eyes. Eyes as green as the rain-washed hills of Ireland. He was all in black. Perhaps that was why he looked so dangerous.

His face was violently handsome – 'violent' was the word that kept ringing in her ears. Slashing cheekbones, lancing black brows, a fierce frown on a mouth that struck her as brutal. His hair was as dark as his clothing and fell in wild waves nearly to his shoulders.

Her heart pounded, a primal warning. Even as she shrank back, she gathered the courage to speak. 'Excuse me. What is it?'

He said nothing. Had been unable to speak since he'd

lifted her off the floor. A trick, a new torment? Was she, after all, only a dream within a dream?

But he'd felt her. The cold damp of her flesh, the weight and the shape of her. Her voice came clear to him now, as did the terror in her eyes.

Why should she be afraid? Why should she fear when she had unmanned him? Five hundred years of solitude hadn't done so, but this woman had accomplished it with one quick stroke.

He stepped closer, his eyes never leaving her face. 'You are come. Why?'

'I ... I don't understand. I'm sorry. Do you speak English?'

One of those arching brows rose. He'd spoken in Gaelic, for he most often thought in the language of his life. But five hundred years of alone had given him plenty of time for linguistics. He could certainly speak English, and half a dozen other languages besides.

'I asked why you have come.'

'I don't know.' She wanted to sit up but was afraid to try it again. 'I think there must have been an accident. I can't quite remember.'

However much it might hurt to move, she couldn't stay flat on her back looking up at him. It made her feel foolish and helpless. She set her teeth, pushed herself up slowly. Her stomach pitched, her head rang, but she managed to sit.

And sitting, glanced around the room.

An enormous room, she noted, and filled with the oddest conglomeration of furnishings. There was an old and beautiful refectory table that held dozens of candlesticks. Silver, wrought iron, pottery, crystal. Pikes were crossed on the wall, and near them was a dramatic painting of the Cliffs of Mohr.

There were display cabinets from various eras. Charles II, James I. Neoclassic bumped up against Venetian, Chippendale against Louis XV. An enormous big-screen television stood near a priceless Victorian davenport.

Placed at random were Waterford bowls, T'ang horses, Dresden vases, and . . . several Pez dispensers.

Despite discomfort, the eccentricity tickled her humor. 'What an interesting room.' She glanced up at him again. He'd yet to stop staring. 'Can you tell me how I got here?'

'You came.'

'Yes, apparently, but how? And . . . I seem to be very wet.'

'It's raining.'

'Oh.' She blew out a breath. The fear had ebbed considerably. After all, the man collected Pez dispensers and Georgian silver. 'I'm sorry, Mister . . . '

'I'm Flynn.'

'Mister Flynn.'

'Flynn,' he repeated.

'All right. I'm sorry, Flynn, I can't seem to think very clearly.' She was shivering, violently now, and wrapped her arms around her chest. 'I was going somewhere, but ... I don't know where I am.'

'Who does?' he murmured. 'You're cold.' And he'd done nothing to tend to her. He would see to her comfort, he decided, and then ... He would simply see.

He scooped her off the couch, faintly irritated when she pushed a hand against his shoulder defensively.

'I'm sure I can walk.'

'I'm more sure I can. You need dry clothes,' he began as he carried her out of the room. 'A warm brew and a hot fire.'

Oh, yes, she thought. It all sounded wonderful. Nearly as wonderful as being carried up a wide, sweeping staircase as if she weighed nothing.

But that was a romantic notion of the kind her mother lived on, the kind that had no place here. She kept that cautious hand pressed to a shoulder that felt like a sculpted curve of rock.

'Thank you for ...' She trailed off. She'd turned her head

21

just a fraction, and now her face was close to his, her eyes only inches from his eyes, her mouth a breath from his mouth. A sharp, unexpected thrill stabbed clean through her heart. The strike was followed by a hard jolt that was something like recognition.

'Do I know you?'

'Wouldn't you have the answer to that?' He leaned in, just a little, breathed. 'Your hair smells of rain.' Even as her eyes went wide, he skimmed his mouth from her jaw-line to her temple. 'And your skin tastes of it.'

He'd learned to savor over the years. To sip even when he wished to gulp. Now he considered her mouth, imagined what flavors her lips would carry. He watched them tremble open.

Ah, yes.

He shifted her, drawing her ever so slightly closer. And she whimpered in pain.

He jerked back, looked down and saw the raw scrape just below her shoulder, and the tear in her sweater. 'You're injured. Why the bloody hell didn't you say so before?'

Out of patience – not his strong suit in any case – he strode into the closest bedchamber, set her down on the side of the bed. In one brisk move he tugged the sweater over her head.

Shocked, she crossed her arms over her breasts. 'Don't you touch me!'

'How can I tend your wounds if I don't touch you?' His brows had lowered, drawn together. She was wearing a bra. He knew they were called that, as he'd seen them worn on the television and in the thin books that were called magazines.

But it was the first time he had witnessed an actual female form so attired.

He liked it very much.

But such delights would have to wait until he saw what condition the woman was in. He leaned over, unhooked her trousers.

'Stop it!' She shoved, tried to scramble back and was hauled not so gently into place.

'Don't be foolish. I've no patience for female flights. If I was after ravishing you, t'would already be done.' Since she continued to struggle, he heaved a breath and looked up.

It was fear he saw – not foolishness but raw fear. A maiden, he thought For God's sake, Flynn, have a care.

'Kayleen.' He spoke quietly now, his voice as soothing as balm on a burn. 'I won't harm you. I only want to see where you're hurt.'

'Are you a doctor?'

23

'Certainly not.'

He seemed so insulted, she nearly laughed.

'I know of healing. Now be still. I ought to have gotten you out of your wet clothes before.' His eyes stayed on hers, seemed to grow brighter. And brighter still, until she could see nothing else. And she sighed. 'Lie back now, there's a lass.'

Mesmerized, she lay on the heaps of silk pillows and, docile as a child, let him undress her.

'Sweet Mary, you've legs that go to forever.' His distraction with them caused the simple spell to waver, and she stirred. 'A man's entitled to the view,' he muttered, then shook his head. 'Look what you've done to yourself. Bruised and scraped one end to the other. Do you like pain, then?'

'No.' Her tongue felt thick. 'Of course not.'

'Some do,' he murmured. He leaned over her again. 'Look at me,' he demanded. 'Look here. Stay.'

Her eyes drooped, half closed as she floated where he wanted, just above the aches. He wrapped her in the quilt, flicked his mind toward the hearth and set the fire roaring.

Then he left her to go to his workshop and gather his potions.

He kept her in the light trance as he tended her. He wanted no maidenly fidgets when he touched her. God, it had been so long since he'd touched a woman, flesh against flesh.

In dreams he'd had her under him, her body eager. He'd laid his lips on her, and his mind had felt her give and arch, her rise, her fall. And so his body had hungered for her.

Now she was here, her lovely skin bruised and chilled.

Now she was here, and didn't know why. Didn't know him.

Despair and desire tangled him in knots.

'Lady, who are you?'

'Kayleen Brennan.'

'Where do you come from?'

'Boston.'

'That's America?'

'Yes.' She smiled. 'It is.'

'Why are you here?'

'I don't know. Where is here?'

'Nowhere. Nowhere at all.'

She reached out, touched his cheek. 'Why are you sad?'

'Kayleen.' Overcome, he gripped her hand, pressed his lips to her palm. 'Do they send you to me so I might know joy again, only to lose it?'

'Who are "they"?'

He lifted his head, felt the fury burn. So he stepped away and turned to stare into the fire.

He could send her deeper, into the dreaming place. There she would remember what there was, would know what she knew. And would tell him. But if there was nothing in her, he wouldn't survive it. Not sane.

He drew a breath. 'I will have my week,' he vowed. 'I will have her before it's done. This I will not cast off. This I will not abjure. You cannot break me with this. Not even with her can you break Flynn.'

He turned back, steady and resolved again. 'The seven days and seven nights are mine, and so is she. What remains here at the last stroke of the last night remains. That is the law. She's mine now.'

Thunder blasted like cannon shot. Ignoring it, he walked to the bed. 'Wake,' he said, and her eyes opened and cleared. As she pushed herself up, he strode to a massive carved armoire, threw the doors open, and selected a long robe of royal blue velvet.

'This will suit you. Dress, then come downstairs.' He tossed the robe on the foot of the bed. 'You'll want food.'

'Thank you, but—'

'We'll talk when you've supped.'

'Yes, but I want—' She hissed in frustration as he walked

out of the room and shut the door behind him with a nasty little slam.

Manners, she thought, weren't high on the list around here. She dragged a hand through her hair, stunned to find it dry again. Impossible. It had been dripping wet when he'd brought her up here only moments before.

She combed her fingers through it again, frowning. Obviously she was mistaken. It must have been all but dry. The accident had shaken her up, confused her. That was why she wasn't remembering things clearly.

She probably needed to go to a hospital, have X-rays taken. Though a hospital seemed silly, really, when she felt fine. In fact, she felt wonderful.

She lifted her arms experimentally. No aches, no twinges. She poked gingerly at the scrape. Hadn't it been longer and deeper along her elbow? It was barely tender now.

Well, she'd been lucky. And now, since she was starving, she'd take the eccentric Flynn up on a meal. After that, her mind was bound to be steadier, and she'd figure out what to do next.

Satisfied, she tossed the covers back. And let out a muffled squeal. She was stark naked.

My God, where were her clothes? She remembered, yes, she remembered the way he'd yanked her sweater off, and then he'd ... Damn it. She pressed a trembling hand to her temple. *Why* couldn't she remember? She'd been frightened, she'd shoved at him, and then ... then she'd been wrapped in a blanket, in a room warmed by a blazing fire and he'd told her to get dressed and come down to dinner.

Well, if she was having blackouts, the hospital was definitely first on the agenda.

She snatched up the robe. Then simply rubbed the rich fabric over her cheek and moaned. It felt like something a princess would wear. Or a goddess. But certainly nothing that Kayleen Brennan of Boston would slip casually into for dinner.

This will suit you, he'd said. The idea of that made her laugh, but she slid her arms into it and let herself enjoy the lustrous warmth against her skin.

She turned, caught her own reflection in a cheval glass. Her hair was a tumble around the shoulders of the deep blue robe that swept down her body and ended in a shimmer of gold lace at the ankles.

I don't look like me, she thought. I look like something out of a fairy tale. Because that made her feel foolish, she turned away.

The bed she'd lain in was covered with velvet as well and lustily canopied with more. On the bureau, and certainly that was a Charles II in perfect condition, sat a lady's brush set of silver with inlays of lapis, antique perfume bottles of opal and of jade. Roses, fresh as morning and white as snow, stood regally in a cobalt vase.

A fairy tale of a room as well, she mused. One fashioned for candlelight and simmering fires. There was a Queen Anne desk in the corner, and tall windows draped in lace and velvet, pretty watercolors of hills and meadows on the walls, lovely faded rugs over the thick planked floors.

If she'd conjured the perfect room, this would have been it.

His manners might be lacking, but his taste was impeccable. Or his wife's, she corrected. For obviously this was a woman's room.

Because the idea should have relieved her, she ignored the little sinking sensation in her belly and satisfied her curiosity by opening the opal bottle.

Wasn't that strange? she thought after a sniff. The bottle held her favorite perfume.

3

Flynn had a stiff whiskey before he dealt with the food. It hit him like a hot fist.

Thank God there were still some things a man could count on.

He would feed his woman – for she was unquestionably his – and he would take some care with her. He would see to her comfort, as a man was meant to do, then he would let her know the way things were to be.

But first he would see that she was steadier on her feet.

The dining hall fireplace was lit. He had the table set with bone china, heavy silver, a pool of fragrant roses, the delicacy of slim white candles and the jewel sparkle of crystal.

Then closing his eyes, lifting his hands palms out, he began to lay the table with the foods that would please her most.

She was so lovely, his Kayleen. He wanted to put the bloom back in her cheeks. He wanted to hear her laugh.

He wanted her.

And so, that was the way things would be.

He stepped back, studied his work with cool satisfaction. Pleased with himself, Flynn went out again to wait at the base of the stairs.

And as she came down toward him, his heart staggered in his chest. '*Speirbhean.*'

Kayleen hesitated. 'I'm sorry?'

'You're beautiful. You should learn the Gaelic,' he said, taking her hand and leading her out of the hall. 'I'll teach you.'

'Well, thank you, but I really don't think that'll be necessary. I really want to thank you, too, for taking me in like this, and I wonder if I might use your phone.' A little detail, Kayleen thought, that had suddenly come to her.

'I have no telephone. Does the gown please you?'

31

'No phone? Well, perhaps one of your neighbors might have one I can use.'

'I have no neighbors.'

'In the closest village,' she said, as panic began to tickle her throat again.

'There is no village. Why are you fretting, Kayleen? You're warm and dry and safe.'

'That may be, but ... how do you know my name?'

'You told me.'

'I don't remember telling you. I don't remember how I—'

'You've no cause to worry. You'll feel better when you've eaten.'

She was beginning to think she had plenty of cause to worry. The well-being she'd felt upstairs in that lovely room was eroding quickly. But when she stepped into the dining room, she felt nothing but shock.

The table was large enough to seat fifty, and spread over it was enough food to feed every one of them.

Bowls and platters and tureens and plates were jammed end to end down the long oak surface. Fruit, fish, meat, soups, a garden of vegetables, an ocean of pastas.

'Where—' Her voice rose, snapped, and had to be fought back under control. 'Where did this come from?'

He sighed. He'd expected delight and instead was given shock. Another thing a man could count on, he thought. Women were forever a puzzle.

'Sit, please. Eat.'

Though she felt little flickers of panic, her voice was calm and firm. 'I want to know where all this food came from. I want to know who else is here. Where's your wife?'

'I have no wife.'

'Don't give me that.' She spun to face him, steady enough now. And angry enough to stand and demand. 'If you don't have a wife, you certainly have a woman.'

'Aye. I have you.'

'Just . . . stay back.' She grabbed a knife from the table, aimed it at him. 'Don't come near me. I don't know what's going on here, and I'm not going to care. I'm going to walk out of this place and keep walking.'

'No.' He stepped forward and neatly plucked what was now a rose from her hand. 'You're going to sit down and eat.'

'I'm in a coma.' She stared at the white rose in his hand, at her own empty one. 'I had an accident. I've hit my head. I'm hallucinating all of this.'

'All of this is real. No one knows better than I the line between what's real and what isn't. Sit down.' He gestured to a chair, swore when she didn't move. 'Have I said I wouldn't harm you? Among my sins has never been a lie or the harm of a woman. Here.' He held out his hand, and now it held the knife. 'Take this, and feel free to use it should I break my word to you.'

'You're . . . ' The knife was solid in her hand. A trick of the eye, she told herself. Just a trick of the eye. 'You're a magician.'

'I am.' His grin was like lightning, fast and bright. Whereas he had been handsome, now he was devastating. His pleasure shone. 'That is what I am, exactly. Sit down, Kayleen, and break fast with me. For I've hungered a long time.'

She took one cautious step in retreat. 'It's too much.'

Thinking she meant the food, he frowned at the table. Considered. 'Perhaps you're right. I got a bit carried away with it all.' He scanned the selections, nodded, then sketched an arch with his hand.

Half the food vanished.

The knife dropped out of her numb fingers. Her eyes rolled straight back.

'Oh, Christ.' It was impatience as much as concern. At least this time he had the wit to catch her before she hit the floor. He sat her in a chair, gave her a little shake, then watched her eyes focus again.

'You didn't understand after all.'

'Understand? Understand?'

'It'll need to be explained, then.' He picked up a plate and began to fill it for her. 'You need to eat or you'll be ill. Your injuries will heal faster if you're strong.'

He set the plate in front of her, began to fill one for himself. 'What do you know of magic, Kayleen Brennan of Boston?'

'It's fun to watch.'

'It can be.'

She would eat, she thought, because she did feel ill. 'And it's an illusion.'

'It can be.' He took the first bite – rare roast beef – and moaned in ecstasy at the taste. The first time he'd come to his week, he'd gorged himself so that he was sick a full day. And had counted it worth it. But now he'd learned to take his time, and appreciate.

'Do you remember now how you came here?'

'It was raining.'

'Yes, and is still.'

'I was going . . . '

'How were you going?'

'How?' She picked up her fork, sampled the fish without thinking. 'I was driving . . . I was driving,' she repeated, on a rising note of excitement. 'Of course. I was

driving, and I was lost. The storm. I was coming from—'
She stopped, struggling through the mists. 'Dublin. I'd
been in Dublin. I'm on vacation. Oh, that's right, I'm on
vacation and I was going to drive around the countryside.
I got lost. Somehow. I was on one of the little roads
through the forest, and it was storming. I could barely see.
Then I . . . '

The relief in her eyes faded as they met his. 'I saw you,'
she whispered. 'I saw you out in the storm.'

'Did you now?'

'You were out in the rain. You said my name. How could
you have said my name before we met?'

She'd eaten little, but he thought a glass of wine might
help her swallow what was to come. He poured it, handed
it to her. 'I've dreamed of you, Kayleen. Dreamed of you for
longer than your lifetime. And dreaming of you I was when
you were lost in my forest. And when I awoke, you'd come.
Do you never dream of me, Kayleen?'

'I don't know what you're talking about. There was a
storm. I was lost. Lightning hit very near, and there was a
deer. A white deer in the road. I swerved to avoid it, and I
crashed. I think I hit a tree. I probably have a concussion, and
I'm imagining things.'

'A white hind.' The humor had gone from his face again.

'You hit a tree with your car? They didn't have to hurt you,' he muttered. 'They had no *right* to hurt you.'

'Who are you talking about?'

'My jailers.' He shoved his plate aside. 'The bloody Keepers.'

'I need to check on my car.' She spoke slowly, calmly. Not just eccentric, she decided. The man was unbalanced. 'Thank you so much for helping me.'

'If you want to check on your car, then we will. In the morning. There's hardly a point in going out in a storm in the middle of the night.' He laid his hand firmly on hers before she could rise. 'You're thinking, "This Flynn, he's lost his mind somewhere along the way." Well, I haven't, though it was a near thing a time or two. Look at me, *leannana*. Do I mean nothing to you?'

'I don't know.' And that was what kept her from bolting. He could look at her, as he was now, and she felt tied to him. Not bound by force, but tied. By her own will. 'I don't understand what you mean, or what's happening to me.'

'Then we'll sit by the fire, and I'll tell you what it all means.' He rose, held out his hand. Irritation washed over his face when she refused to take it. 'Do you want the knife?'

She glanced down at it, back up at him. 'Yes.'

'Then bring it along with you.'

He plucked up the wine, and the glasses, and led the way.

He sat by the fire, propped his boots on the hearth, savored his wine and the scent of the woman who sat so warily beside him. 'I was born in magic,' he began. 'Some are. Others apprentice and can learn well enough. But to be born in it is more a matter of controlling the art than of learning it.'

'So your father was a magician.'

'No, he was a tailor. Magic doesn't have to come down through the blood. It simply has to *be* in the blood.' He paused because he didn't want to blunder again. He should know more of her, he decided, before he did. 'What is it you are, back in your Boston?'

'I'm an antique dealer. That came through the blood. My uncles, my grandfather, and so on. Brennan's of Boston has been doing business for nearly a century.'

'Nearly a century, is it?' he chuckled. 'So very long.'

'I suppose it doesn't seem so by European standards. But America's a young country. You have some magnificent pieces in your home.'

'I collect what appeals to me.'

'Apparently a wide range appeals to you. I've never seen such a mix of styles and eras in one place before.'

He glanced around the room, considering. It wasn't something he'd thought of, but he'd had only himself to please up until now. 'You don't like it?'

Because it seemed to matter to him, she worked up a smile. 'No, I like it very much. In my business I see a lot of beautiful and interesting pieces, and I've always felt it was a shame more people don't just toss them together and make their own style rather than sticking so rigidly to a pattern. No one can accuse you of sticking to a pattern.'

'No. That's a certainty.'

She started to curl up her legs, caught herself. What in the world was wrong with her? She was relaxing into an easy conversation with what was very likely a madman. She cut her gaze toward the knife beside her, then back to him. And found him studying her contemplatively.

'I wonder if you could use it. There are two kinds of people in the world, don't you think? Those who fight and those who flee. Which are you, Kayleen?'

'I've never been in the position where I had to do either.'

'That's either fortunate or tedious. I'm not entirely sure which. I like a good fight myself,' he added with that quick grin. 'Just one of my many flaws. Fact is, I miss going fist to fist with a man. I miss a great many things.'

'Why? Why do you have to miss anything?'

'That's the point, isn't it, of this fireside conversation. The why. Are you wondering, *mavourneen*, if I'm off in my head?'

'Yes,' she said, then immediately froze.

'I'm not, though perhaps it would've been easier if I'd gone a bit crazy along the way. They knew I had a strong mind – part of the problem, in their thinking, and part of the reason for the sentence weighed on me.'

'They?' Her fingers inched toward the handle of the knife. She could use it, she promised herself. She *would* use it if she had to, no matter how horribly sad and lonely he looked.

'The Keepers. The ancient and the revered who guard and who nurture magic. And have done so since the Waiting Time, when life was no more than the heavens taking their first breath.'

'Gods?' she said cautiously.

'In some ways of thinking.' He was brooding again, frowning into the flames. 'I was born of magic, and when I was old enough I left my family to do the work. To heal and to help. Even to entertain. Some of us have more of a knack, you could say, for the fun of it.'

'Like, um, sawing a lady in half.'

He looked at her with a mixture of amusement and exasperation. 'This is illusion, Kayleen.'

'Yes.'

'I speak of magic, not pretense. Some prophesy, some travel and study, for the sake of it. Others devote their art to healing body or soul. Some choose to make a living performing. Some might serve a worthy master, as Merlin did Arthur. There are as many choices as there are people. And while none may choose to harm or profit for the sake of it, all are real.'

He slipped a long chain from under his shirt, held the pendant with its milky stone out for her to see. 'A moonstone,' he told her. 'And the words around are my name, and my title. *Draiodoir*. Magician.'

'It's beautiful.' Unable to resist, she curved her hand around the pendant. And felt a bolt of heat, like the rush of a comet, spurt from her fingertips to her toes. 'God!'

Before she could snatch her hand away, Flynn closed his own over hers. 'Power,' he murmured. 'You feel it. Can all but taste it. A seductive thing. And inside, you can make yourself think there's nothing impossible. Look at me, Kayleen.'

She already was, could do nothing else. Wanted nothing

else. There you are, she thought again. There you are, at last.

'I could have you now. You would willingly lie with me now, as you have in dreams. Without fear. Without questions.'

'Yes.'

And his need was a desperate thing, leaping, snapping at the tether of control. 'I want more.' His fingers tightened on hers. 'What is it in you that makes me crave more, when I don't know what more is? Well, we've time to find the answer. For now, I'll tell you a story. A young magician left his family. He traveled and he studied. He helped and he healed. He had pride in his work, in himself. Some said too much pride.'

He paused now, thinking, for there had been times in this last dreaming that he'd wondered if that could be so.

'His skill, this magician's, was great, and he was known in his world. Still, he was a man, with the needs of a man, the desires of a man, the faults of a man. Would you want a man perfect, Kayleen?'

'I want you.'

'*Leannana*.' He leaned over, pressed his lips to her knuckles. 'This man, this magician, he saw the world. He read its books, listened to its music. He came and went as he pleased, did as he pleased. Perhaps he was careless on occasion, and though he did no harm, neither did he heed the rules and the warnings he was given. The power was so strong in him, what need had he for rules?'

'Everyone needs rules. They keep us civilized.'

'Do you think?' It amused him how prim her voice had become. Even held by the spell, she had a strong mind, and a strong will. 'We'll discuss that sometime. But for now, to continue the tale. He came to know a woman. Her beauty was blinding, her manner sweet. He believed her to be innocent. Such was his romantic nature.'

'Did you love her?'

'Yes, I loved her. I loved the angel-faced, innocent maid I saw when I looked at her. I asked for her hand, for it wasn't just a tumble I wanted from her but a lifetime. And when I asked, she wept, ah, pretty tears down a smooth cheek. She couldn't be mine, she told me, as much as her heart already was. For there was a man, a wealthy man, a cruel man, who had contracted for her. Her father had sold her, and her fate was sealed.'

'You couldn't let that happen.'

'Ah, you see that, too.' It pleased him that she saw it, stood with him on that vital point. 'No, how could I let her go loveless to another? To be sold like a horse in the marketplace? I would take her away, I said, and she wept the more.

43

I would give her father twice what had been given, and she sobbed upon my shoulder. It could not be done, for then surely the man would kill her poor father, or see him in prison, or some horrible fate. So long as the man had his wealth and position, her family would suffer. She couldn't bear to be the cause of it, even though her heart was breaking.'

Kayleen shook her head, frowned. 'I'm sorry, but that doesn't make sense. If the money was paid back and her father was wealthy now, he could certainly protect himself, and he would have the law to—'

'The heart doesn't follow such reason,' he interrupted, impatiently because if he'd had the wit in his head at the time, instead of fire in his blood, he'd have come to those same conclusions. 'It was saving her that was my first thought – and my last. Protecting her, and yes, perhaps, by doing so having her love me the more. I would take this cruel man's wealth and his position from him. I vowed this, and oh, how her eyes shone, diamonds of tears. I would take what he had and lay it at her feet. She would live like a queen, and I would care for her all my life.'

'But stealing—'

'Will you just listen?' Exasperation hissed through his voice.

'Of course.' Her chin lifted, a little tilt of resentment 'I beg your pardon.'

'So this I did, whistling the wind, drawing down the moon, kindling the cold fire. This I did, and did freely for her. And the man woke freezing in a crofter's cot instead of his fine manor house. He woke in rags instead of his warm nightclothes. I took his life from him, without spilling a drop of blood. And when it was done, I stood in the smoldering dark of that last dawn, triumphant.'

He fell into silence a moment, and when he continued, his voice was raw. 'The Keepers encased me in a shield of crystal, holding me there as I cursed them, as I shouted my protests, as I used the heart and innocence of my young maid as my defense for my crime. And they showed me how she laughed as she gathered the wealth I'd sent to her, as she leapt into a carriage laden with it and fell into the arms of the lover with whom she'd plotted the ruin of the man she hated. And my ruin as well.'

'But you loved her.'

'I did, but the Keepers don't count love as an excuse, as a reason. I was given a choice. They would strip me of my power, take away what was in my blood and make me merely human. Or I would keep it, and live alone, in a half world, without companionship, without human contact, without the pleasures of the world that I, in their estimation, had betrayed.'

'That's cruel. Heartless.'

'So I claimed, but it didn't sway them. I took the second choice, for they would not empty me. I would not abjure my birthright. Here I have existed, since that night of betrayal, a hundred years times five, with only one week each century to feel as a man does again.

'I am a man, Kayleen.' With his hand still gripping hers, he got to his feet. Drew her up. 'I am,' he murmured, sliding his free hand into her hair, fisting it there.

He lowered his head, his lips nearly meeting hers, then hesitated. The sound of her breath catching, releasing, shivered through him. She trembled under his hand, and he felt, inside himself, the stumble of her heart.

'Quietly this time,' he murmured. 'Quietly.' And brushed his lips, a whisper, once ... twice over hers. The flavor bloomed inside him like a first sip of fine wine.

He drank slowly. Even when her lips parted, invited, he drank slowly. Savoring the texture of her mouth, the easy slide of tongues, the faint, faint scrape of teeth.

Her body fit against his, so lovely, so perfect. The heat from the moonstone held between their hands spread like sunlight and began to pulse.

So even drinking slowly he was drunk on her.

When he drew back, her sigh all but shattered him.

'*A ghra.*' Weak, wanting, he lowered his brow to hers. With a sigh of his own he tugged the pendant free. Her eyes, soft, loving, clouded, began to clear. Before the change was complete, he pressed his mouth to hers one last time.

'Dream,' he said.

4

She woke to watery sunlight and the heady scent of roses. There was a low fire simmering in the grate and a silk pillow under her head.

Kayleen stirred and rolled over to snuggle in.

Then shot up in bed like an arrow from a plucked bow.

My God, it had really happened. All of it.

And for lord's sake, for *lord's* sake, she was naked again.

Had he given her drugs, hypnotized her, gotten her drunk? What other reason could there be for her to have slept like a baby – and naked as one – in a bed in the house of a crazy man?

Instinctively, she snatched at the sheets to cover herself, and then she saw the single white rose.

An incredibly sweet, charmingly romantic crazy man, she thought and picked up the rose before she could resist.

That story he'd told her – magic and betrayal and five hundred years of punishment. He'd actually believed it. Slowly she let out a breath. So had she. She'd sat there, listening and believing every word – then. Hadn't seen a single thing odd about it, but had felt sorrow and anger on his behalf. Then . . .

He'd kissed her, she remembered. She pressed her fingertips to her lips, stunned at her own behavior. The man had kissed her, had made her feel like rich cream being gently lapped out of a bowl. More, she'd *wanted* him to kiss her. Had wanted a great deal more than that.

And perhaps, she thought, dragging the sheets higher, there had been a great deal more than that.

She started to leap out of bed, then changed her mind and crept out instead. She had to get away, quickly and quietly. And to do so, she needed clothes.

She tiptoed to the wardrobe, wincing at the creak as she eased the door open. It was one more shock to look inside and see silks and velvets, satins and lace, all in rich, bold colors. Such beautiful things. The kind of clothes she would covet but never buy. So impractical, so frivolous, really.

So gorgeous.

Shaking her head at her foolishness, she snatched out her own practical trousers, her torn sweater . . . but it wasn't torn. Baffled, she turned it over, inside out, searching for the jagged rip in the arm. It wasn't there.

She hadn't imagined that tear. She couldn't have imagined it. Because she was beginning to shake, she dragged it over her head, yanked the trousers on. Trousers that were pristine, though they had been stained and muddy.

She dove into the wardrobe, pushing through evening slippers, kid boots, and found her simple black flats. Flats that should have been well worn, caked with dirt, scarred just a little on the inside left where she had knocked against a chest the month before in her shop.

But the shoes were unmarked and perfect, as if they'd just come out of the box.

She would think about it later. She'd think about it all later. Now she had to get away from here, away from him. Away from whatever was happening to her.

Her knees knocked together as she crept to the door, eased it open, and peeked out into the hallway. She saw beautiful rugs on a beautiful floor, paintings and tapestries on the walls, more doors, all closed. And no sign of Flynn.

She slipped out, hurrying as quickly as she dared. Wild with relief, she bolted down the stairs, raced to the door, yanked it open with both hands.

And barreling through, ran straight into Flynn.

'Good morning.' He grasped her shoulders, steadying her even as he thought what a lovely thing it would be if she'd been running toward him instead of away from him. 'It seems we've done with the rain for now.'

'I was – I just—' Oh, God. 'I want to go check on my car.'

'Of course. You may want to wait till the mists burn off. Would you like your breakfast?'

'No, no.' She made her lips curve. 'I'd really like to see how badly I damaged the car. So, I'll just go see and . . . let you know.'

'Then I'll take you to it.'

'No, really.'

But he turned away, whistled. He took her hand, ignoring her frantic tugs for release, and led her down the steps.

Out of the mists came a white horse at the gallop, the charger of folklore with his mane flying, his silver bridle ringing. Kayleen managed one short shriek as he arrowed toward them, powerful legs shredding the mists, magnificent head tossing.

He stopped inches from Flynn's feet, blew softly, then nuzzled Flynn's chest.

With a laugh, Flynn threw his arms around the horse's neck. With the same joy, she thought, that a boy might embrace a beloved dog. He spoke to the horse in low tones, crooning ones, in what she now recognized as Gaelic.

Still grinning, Flynn eased back. He lifted a hand, flicked the wrist, and the palm that had been empty now held a glossy red apple. 'No, I would never forget. There's for my beauty,' he said, and the horse dipped his head and nipped the apple neatly out of Flynn's palm.

'His name is Dilis. It means faithful, and he is.' With economical and athletic grace, Flynn vaulted into the saddle, held down a hand for Kayleen.

'Thank you all the same, and he's very beautiful, but I don't know how to ride. I'll just—' The words slid back down her throat as Flynn leaned down, gripped her arm, and pulled her up in front of him as though she weighed less than a baby.

'I know how to ride,' he assured her and tapped Dilis lightly with his heels.

The horse reared, and Kayleen's scream mixed with

Flynn's laughter as the fabulous beast pawed the air. Then they were leaping forward and flying into the forest.

There was nothing to do but hold on. She banded her arms around Flynn, buried her face in his chest. It was insane, absolutely insane. She was an ordinary woman who led an ordinary life. How could she be galloping through some Irish forest on a great white horse, plastered against a man who claimed to be a fifteenth-century magician?

It had to stop, and it had to stop now.

She lifted her head, intending to tell him firmly to rein his horse in, to let her off and let her go. And all she did was stare. The sun was slipping in fingers through the arching branches of the trees. The air glowed like polished pearls.

Beneath her the horse ran fast and smooth at a breathless, surely a reckless, pace. And the man who rode him was the most magnificent man she'd ever seen.

His dark hair flew, his eyes glittered. And that sadness he carried, which was somehow its own strange appeal, had lifted. What she saw on his face was joy, excitement, delight, challenge. A dozen things, and all of them strong.

And seeing them, her heart beat as fast as the horse's hooves. 'Oh, my God!'

It wasn't possible to fall in love with a stranger. It didn't happen in the real world.

Weakly, she let her head fall back to his chest. But maybe it was time to admit, or at least consider, that she'd left the real world the evening before when she'd taken that wrong turn into the forest.

Dilis slowed to a canter, stopped. Once again, Kayleen lifted her head. This time her eyes met Flynn's. This time he read what was in them. As the pleasure of it rose in him, he leaned toward her.

'No. Don't.' She lifted her hand, pressed it to his lips. 'Please.'

His nod was curt. 'As you wish.' He leapt off the horse, plucked her down. 'It appears your mode of transportation is less reliable than mine,' he said, and turned her around.

The car had smashed nearly headlong into an oak. The oak, quite naturally, had won the bout. The hood was buckled back like an accordion, the safety glass a surrealistic pattern of cracks. The air bag had deployed, undoubtedly saving her from serious injury. She'd been driving too fast for the conditions, she remembered. Entirely too fast.

But how had she been driving at all?

That was the question that struck her now. There was no road. The car sat broken on what was no more than a footpath through the forest. Trees crowded in everywhere, along with brambles and wild vines that bloomed with unearthly flowers. And when she slowly turned in a circle, she saw no route she could have maneuvered through them in the rain, in the dark.

She saw no tracks from her tires in the damp ground. There was no trace of her journey; there was only the end of it.

Cold, she hugged her arms. Her sweater, she thought, wasn't ripped. Cautiously, she pushed up the sleeve, and there, where she'd been badly scraped and bruised, her skin was smooth and unmarred.

She looked back at Flynn. He stood silently as his horse idly cropped at the ground. Temper was in his eyes, and she could all but see the sparks of impatience shooting off him.

Well, she had a temper of her own if she was pushed far enough. And her own patience was at an end. 'What is this place?' she demanded, striding up to him. 'Who the hell are you, and what have you done? How have you done it? How the devil can I be here when I can't possibly be here? That car—' She flung her hand out. 'I couldn't have driven it here. I couldn't have.' Her arm dropped limply to her side. 'How could I?'

'You know what I told you last night was the truth.'

She did know. With her anger burned away, she did know it. 'I need to sit down.'

55

'The ground's damp.' He caught her arm before she could just sink to the floor of the forest. 'Here, then.' And he lowered her gently into a high-backed chair with a plump cushion of velvet.

'Thank you.' She began to laugh, and burying her face in her hands, shook with it. 'Thank you very much. I've lost my mind. Completely lost my mind.'

'You haven't. But it would help us both considerably if you'd open it a bit.'

She lowered her hands. She was not a hysterical woman, and would not become one. She no longer feared him. However savagely handsome his looks, he'd done her no harm. The fact was, he'd tended to her.

But facts were the problem, weren't they? The fact that she couldn't be here, but was. That he couldn't exist, yet did. The fact that she felt what she felt, without reason.

Once upon a time, she thought, then drew a long breath.

'I don't believe in fairy tales.'

'Now, then, that's very sad. Why wouldn't you? Do you think any world can exist without magic? Where does the color come from, and the beauty? Where are the miracles?'

'I don't know. I don't have any answers. Either I'm having a very complex dream or I'm sitting in the woods in a' – she got to her feet to turn and examine the chair – 'a marquetry side chair, Dutch, I believe, early eighteenth century. Very nice. Yes, well.' She sat again. 'I'm sitting here in this beautiful chair in a forest wrapped in mists, having ridden here on that magnificent horse, after having spent the night in a castle—'

''Tisn't a castle, really. More a manor.'

'Whatever, with a man who claims to be more than five hundred years old.'

'Five hundred and twenty-eight, if we're counting.'

'Really? You wear it quite well. A five-hundred-and-twenty-eight-year-old magician who collects Pez dispensers.'

'Canny little things.'

'And I don't know how any of it can be true, but I believe it. I believe all of it. Because continuing to deny what I see with my own eyes makes less sense than believing it.'

'There.' He beamed at her. 'I knew you were a sensible woman.'

'Oh, yes, I'm very sensible, very steady. So I have to believe what I see, even if it's irrational.'

'If that which is rational exists, that which is irrational must as well. There is ever a balance to things, Kayleen.'

'Well.' She sat calmly, glancing around. 'I believe in balance.' The air sparkled. She could feel it on her face. She could smell the deep, dark richness of the woods. She could hear the trill of birdsong. She was where she was, and so was he.

'So, I'm sitting in this lovely chair in an enchanted forest having a conversation with a five-hundred-and-twenty-eight-year-old magician. And, if all that isn't crazy enough, there's one more thing that tops it all off. I'm in love with him.'

The easy smile on his face faded. What ran through him was so hot and tangled, so full of layers and routes he couldn't breathe through it all. 'I've waited for you, through time, through dreams, through those small windows of life that are as much torture as treasure. Will you come to me now, Kayleen? Freely?'

She got to her feet, walked across the soft cushion of forest floor to him. 'I don't know how I can feel like this. I only know I do.'

He pulled her into his arms, and this time the kiss was hungry. Possessive. When she pressed her body to his, wound her arms around his neck, he deepened the kiss, took more. Filled himself with her.

Her head spun, and she reveled in the giddiness. No one had ever wanted her – not like this. Had ever touched her like this. Needed her. Desire was a hot spurt that fired the blood and made logic, reason, sanity laughable things.

She had magic. What did she need of reason?

'Mine.' He murmured it against her mouth. Said it again and again as his lips raced over her face, her throat. Then, throwing his head back, he shouted it.

'She's mine now and ever. I claim her, as is my right.'

When he lifted her off her feet, lightning slashed across the sky. The world trembled.

They rode through the forest. He showed her a stream where golden fish swam over silver rocks. Where a waterfall tumbled down into a pool clear as blue glass.

He stopped to pick her wildflowers and thread them through her hair. And when he kissed her, it was soft and sweet.

His moods, she thought, were as magical as the rest of him, and just as inexplicable. He courted her, making her laugh as he plucked baubles out of thin air and painted rainbows in the sky.

She could feel the breeze on her cheeks, smell the flowers and the damp. What was in her heart was like music. Fairy tales *were* real, she thought. All the years she'd turned her back on them, dismissed the happily-ever-after that her mother sighed over, her own magic had been waiting for her.

Nothing would ever, could ever, be the same again.

Had she known it somehow? Deep inside, had she known it had only been waiting, that he had only been waiting for her to awake?

They walked or rode while birds chorused around them and mists faded away into brilliant afternoon.

There beside the pool he laid a picnic, pouring wine out of his open hand to amuse her. Touching her hair, her cheek, her shoulders dozens of times, as if the contact was as much reassurance as flirtation.

She'd never had a romance. Never taken the time for one. Now it seemed a lifetime of love and anticipation could be fit into one perfect day.

He knew something about everything. History, culture, art, literature, science. It was a new thrill to realize that the man who held her heart, who attracted her so completely, appealed to her mind as well. He could make her laugh, make her wonder, make her yearn. And he brought her a contentment she hadn't known she'd lived without.

If this was a dream, she thought, as twilight fell and they mounted the horse once more, she hoped never to wake.

5

A perfect day deserved a perfect night. She had thought, hoped, that when they returned from their outing, he would take her inside. Take her to bed.

But he had only kissed her in that stirring way that made her weak and jittery and asked if she might like to change for the evening.

So she had gone up to her room to worry and wonder how a woman prepared, after the most magical of days, for the most momentous night of her life. Of one thing she was certain. It wouldn't do to think. If she let her thoughts take shape, the doubts would creep in. Doubts about every-thing that had happened – and about what would happen yet

For once, she would simply act. She would simply be.

The bath that adjoined her room was a testament to modern luxury. Stepping from the bedchamber with its antiques and plush velvets into this sea of tile and glass was like stepping from one world into another.

Which was, she supposed, something she'd done already. She filled the huge tub with water and scent and oil, let the low hum of the motor and quiet jets relax her as she sank in up to her chin.

Silver-topped pots sat on the long white counter. From them she scooped out cream to smooth over her skin. And watched herself in the steam-hazed window. This was the way women had prepared for a lover for centuries. Scenting and softening themselves for a man's hands. For a man's mouth.

A woman's magic.

She wouldn't be afraid, she wouldn't let anxiety crowd out the pleasure.

In the wardrobe she found a long gown of silk in the color of ripe plums. It slid over her body like sin and scooped low over her breasts. She slipped her feet into silver slippers, started to turn to the glass.

No, she thought, she didn't want to see herself reflected in a mirror. She wanted to see herself reflected in Flynn's eyes.

He felt like a green youth, all eager nerves and awkward moves. In his day, he'd had quite a way with the ladies. Though five hundred years could certainly make a man rusty in certain areas, he'd had dreams.

But even in dreams, he hadn't wanted so much.

How could he? he thought as Kayleen started down the staircase toward him. Dreams paled next to the power of her.

He reached out, almost afraid that his hand would pass through her and leave him nothing but this yearning. 'You're the most beautiful woman I've ever known.'

'Tonight' – she linked her fingers with his – 'everything's beautiful.' She stepped toward him and was confused when he stepped back.

'I thought . . . Will you dance with me, Kayleen?'

As he spoke, the air filled with music. Candles, hundreds of them, spurted into flame. The light was pale gold now, and flowers blossomed down the walls, turning the hall into a garden.

'I'd love to,' she said, and moved into his arms.

They waltzed in the Great Hall, through the swaying candle-light and the perfume of roses that bloomed everywhere. Doors and windows sprang open, welcoming the glow of moon and stars and die fragrance of the night.

Thrilled, Kayleen threw back her head and let him sweep her in stirring circles. 'It's wonderful! Everything's wonderful. How can you know how to waltz like this when there was no waltz in your time?'

'Watching through dreams. I see the world go by in them, and I take what pleases me most. I've danced with you in dreams, Kayleen. You don't remember?'

'No,' she whispered. 'I don't dream. And if I do, I never remember. But I'll remember this.' She smiled at him. 'Forever.'

'You're happy.'

'I've never in my life been so happy.' Her hand slid from his shoulder, along his neck, to rest on his cheek. The blue of her eyes deepened. Went dreamy. 'Flynn.'

'Wine,' he said, when fresh nerves kicked in his belly. 'You'll want wine.'

'No.' The music continued to swell as they stood. 'I don't want wine.'

'Supper, then.'

'No.' Her hand trailed over, cupped the back of his neck. 'Not supper either,' she murmured and drew his mouth to hers. 'You.' She breathed it. 'Only you.'

'Kayleen.' He'd intended to romance her, charm her. Seduce her. Now she had done all of that to him. 'I don't want to rush you.'

'I've waited so long, without even knowing. There's never been anyone else. Now I think there couldn't have been, because there was you. Show me what it's like to belong.'

'There's no woman I've touched who mattered. They're shadows beside you, Kayleen. This,' he said and lifted her into his arms, 'is real.'

He carried her through the music and candlelight, up the grand stairs. And though she felt his arms, the beat of his heart, it was like floating.

'Here is where I dreamed of you in the night.' He took her into his bedchamber, where the bed was covered with red silk and the petals of white roses, where candles stood flaming and the fire shimmered. 'And here is where I'll love you, this first time. Flesh to flesh.'

He set her on her feet. 'I won't hurt you, that I can prom-ise. I'll give you only pleasure.'

'I'm not afraid.'

'Then be with me.' He cupped her face in his hands, laid his lips on hers.

In dreams there had been longing, and echoes of sensations. Here and now, with those mists parted, there was so much more.

Gently, so gently, his mouth took from hers. Warmth and wanting. With tenderness and patience, his hands moved over her. Soft and seductive. When she trembled, he soothed, murmuring her name, and promises. He slid the gown off her shoulders, trailed kisses over that curve of flesh. And thrilled to the flavor and the fragrance.

'Let me see you now, lovely Kayleen.' He skimmed his lips along her throat as he eased the gown down her body. When it pooled at her feet, he stepped back and looked his fill.

There was no shyness in her. The heat that rose up to bloom on her skin was anticipation. The tremble that danced through her was delight when his gaze finished its journey and his eyes locked on hers.

He reached out, caressed the curve of her breast, let them both absorb the sensation. When his fingertips trailed down, he felt her quiver under his touch.

She reached for him, her hands not quite steady as she unbuttoned his shirt. And when she touched him, it was like freedom.

'*A ghra.*' He pulled her against him, crushed her mouth with his, lost himself in the needs that stormed through him. His hands raced over her, took, sought more, until she gasped out his name.

Too fast, too much. God help him. He fought back through the pounding in his blood, gentled his movements, chained the raw need. When he lifted her again, laid her on the bed, his kiss was long and slow and gentle.

This, she thought, was what the poets wrote of. This was why a man or a woman would reject reason for even the chance of love.

This warmth, this pleasure of another's body against your own. This gift of heart, and all the sighs and secrets it offered.

He gave her pleasure, as he had promised, drowning floods of it that washed through her in slow waves. She could have lain steeped in it forever.

She gave to him a taste, a touch, so that sensation pillowed the aches. He savored, and lingered, and held fast to the beauty she offered.

When flames licked at the edges of warmth, she welcomed them. The pretty clouds that had cushioned her began to thin. Falling through them, she cried out. A sound of triumph as her heart burst inside her.

And heard him moan, heard the quick whispers, a kind of incantation as he rose over her. Through the candlelight and the shimmer of her own vision she saw his face, his eyes. So green now they were like dark jewels. Swamped with love, she laid a hand on his cheek, murmured his name.

'Look at me. Aye, at me.' His breath wanted to tear out of his lungs. His body begged to plunge. 'Only pleasure.'

He took her innocence, filled her, and gave her the joy. She opened for him, rose with him, her eyes swimming with shocked delight. And with the love he craved like breath.

And this time, when she fell, he gathered himself and plunged after her.

Her body shimmered. She was certain that if she looked in the mirror she would see it was golden. And his, she thought, trailing a hand lazily up and down his back. His was so beautiful. Strong and hard and smooth.

His heart was thundering against hers still. What a fantastic sensation that was, to be under the weight of the man you loved and feel his heart race for you.

Perhaps that was why her mother kept searching, kept risking. For this one moment of bliss. Love, Kayleen thought, changes everything.

And she loved.

Was loved. She repeated that over and over in her head. She was loved. It didn't matter that he hadn't said it, in those precise words. He couldn't look at her as he did, couldn't touch her as he did and not love her.

A woman didn't change her life, believe in spells and fairy tales after years of denial, and not be given the happy ending.

Flynn loved her. That was all she needed to know.

'Why do you worry?'

She blinked herself back. 'What?'

'I feel it. Inside you.' He lifted his head and studied her face. 'The worry.'

'No. It's only that everything's different now. So much is happening to me in so little time.' She brushed her fingers through his hair and smiled. 'But it's not worry.'

'I want your happiness, Kayleen.'

'I know.' And wasn't that love, after all? 'I know.' And laughing, she threw her arms around him. 'And you have it. You make me ridiculously happy.'

'There's often not enough ridiculous in a life.' He pulled her up with him so they were sitting tangled together on silk roses. 'So let's have a bit.'

The stone in his pendant glowed brighter as he grinned. He fisted his hands, shot them open.

In a wink the bed around them was covered with platters of food and bottles of wine. It made her jolt. She wondered if such things always would. Angling her head, she lifted a glass.

'I'd rather champagne, if you please.'

'Well, then.'

She watched the glass fill, bottom to top, with the frothy wine. And laughing, she toasted him and drank it down.

6

All of her life Kayleen had done the sensible thing. As a child, she'd tidied her room without being reminded, studied hard in school and turned in all assignments in a timely fashion. She had grown into a woman who was never late for an appointment, spent her money wisely, and ran the family business with a cool, clear head.

Looking back through the veil of what had been, Kayleen decided she had certainly been one of the most tedious people on the face of the planet.

How could she have known there was such freedom in doing the ridiculous or the impulsive or the foolish?

She said as much to Flynn as she lay sprawled over him on the bed of velvety flowers.

'You couldn't be tedious.'

'Oh, but I could.' She lifted her head from his chest. She wore nothing but her smile, with its dimple, and flowers in her hair. 'I was the queen of tedium. I set my alarm for six o'clock every morning, even when I didn't have to get up for work. I even set alarms when I was on vacation.'

'Because you didn't want to miss anything.'

'No. Because one must maintain discipline. I walked to work every day, rain or shine, along the exact same route. This was after making my bed and eating a balanced breakfast, of course.'

She slithered down so that she could punctuate her words with little kisses over his shoulders and chest. 'I arrived at the shop precisely thirty minutes before opening, in order to see to the morning paperwork and check any displays that might require updating. Thirty minutes for a proper lunch, fifteen minutes, exactly, at four for a cup of tea, then close shop and walk home by that same route.'

She worked her way up his throat. 'Mmmm. Watched the news during dinner – must keep up with current affairs.

Read a chapter of a good book before bed. Except for Wednesdays. Wednesdays I went wild and took in an interesting film. And on my half day, I would go over to my mother's to lecture her.'

Though her pretty mouth was quite a distraction, he paid attention to her words, and the tone of them. 'You lectured your mother?'

'Oh, yes.' She nibbled at his ear. 'My beautiful, frivolous, delightful mother. How I must have irritated her. She's been married three times, engaged double that, at least. It never works out, and she's heartbroken about it for, oh, about an hour and a half.'

With a laugh, Kayleen lifted her head again. 'That's not fair, of course, but she manages to shake it all off and never lose her optimism about love. She forgets to pay her bills, misses appointments, never knows the correct time, and has never been known to be able to find her keys. She's wonderful.'

'You love her very much.'

'Yes, very much.' Sighing now, Kayleen pillowed her head on Flynn's shoulder. 'I decided when I was very young that it was my job to take care of her. That was after her husband number two.'

He combed his fingers through her flower-bedecked hair. 'Did you lose your father?'

'No, but you could say he lost us. He left us when I was six. I suppose you could call him frivolous, too, which was yet another motivation for me to be anything but. He never settled into the family business well. Or into marriage, or into fatherhood. I hardly remember him.'

He stroked her hair, said nothing. But he was beginning to worry. 'Were you happy, in that life?'

'I wasn't unhappy. Brennan's was important to me, maybe all the more so because it wasn't important to my father. He shrugged off the tradition of it, the responsibility of it, as carelessly as he shrugged off his wife and his daughter.'

'And hurt you.'

'At first. Then I stopped letting it hurt me.'

Did you? Flynn wondered. Or is that just one more pretense?

'I thought everything had to be done a certain way to be done right. If you do things right, people don't leave,' she said softly. 'And you'll know exactly what's going to happen next. My uncle and grandfather gradually let me take over the business because I had a knack for it, and they were proud of that. My mother let me handle things at home because, well, she's just too good-natured not to.'

She sighed again, snuggled into him. 'She's going to get married again next month, and she's thrilled. One of the reasons I took this trip now is because I wanted to get away from it, from those endless plans for yet another of her happy endings. I suppose I hurt her feelings, leaving the way I did. But I'd have hurt them more if I'd stayed and spoke my mind.'

'You don't like the man she'll marry?'

'No, he's perfectly nice. My mother's fiancés are always perfectly nice. Funny, since I've been here I haven't worried about her at all. And I imagine, somehow, she's managing just fine without me picking at her. The shop's undoubtedly running like clockwork, and the world continues to spin. Odd to realize I wasn't indispensable after all.'

'To me you are.' He wrapped his arms around her, rolled over so he could look down at her. 'You're vital to me.'

'That's the most wonderful thing anyone's ever said to me.' It was better, wasn't it? she asked herself. Even better than 'I love you.' 'I don't know what time it is, or even what day. I don't need to know. I've never eaten supper in bed unless I was ill. Never danced in a forest in the moonlight, never made love in a bed of flowers. I've never known what it was like to be so free.'

'Happy, Kayleen.' He took her mouth, a little desperately. 'You're happy.'

'I love you, Flynn. How could I be happier?'

He wanted to keep her loving him. Keep her happy. He wanted to keep her beautifully naked and steeped in pleasures.

More than anything, he wanted to keep her.

The hours were whizzing by so quickly, tumbling into days so that he was losing track of time himself. What did time matter now, to either of them?

He could give her anything she wanted here. Anything and everything. What would she miss of the life she had outside? It was ordinary and tedious. Hadn't she said so herself? He would see that she never missed what had been. Before long she wouldn't even think of it. The life before would be the dream.

He taught her to ride, and she was fearless. When he thought of how she'd clung to him in terror when he'd pulled her up onto Dilis the first time, he rationalized the change by saying she was simply quick to learn. He hadn't changed her basic nature, or forced her will.

That was beyond his powers and the most essential rule of magic.

When she galloped off into the forest, her laughter streaming behind her, he told himself he let his mind follow her only to keep her from harm.

Yet he knew, deep inside himself, that if she traveled near the edge of his world, he would pull her back.

He had that right, Flynn thought, as his hands fisted at his sides. He had claimed her. What he claimed during his imprisonment was his to keep.

'That is the law.' He threw his head back, scowling up at the heavens. 'It is *your* law. She came to me. By rights of magic, by the law of this place, she is mine. No power can take her from me.'

When the sky darkened, when lightning darted at the black edges of clouds, Flynn stood in the whistling wind, feet planted in challenge. His hair blew wild around his face, his eyes went emerald-bright. And the power that was his, that could not be taken from him, shimmered around him like silver.

In his mind he saw Kayleen astride the white horse. She glanced uneasily at the gathering storm, shivered in the fresh chill of the wind. And turned her mount to ride back to him.

She was laughing again as she raced out of the trees. 'That was wonderful!' She threw her arms recklessly in the air so that Flynn gripped the halter to keep Dilis steady. 'I want to ride every day. I can't believe the *feeling*.'

Feeling, he thought with a vicious tug of guilt, was the one thing he wouldn't be able to offer her much longer.

'Come, darling.' He lifted his arms up to her. 'We'll put Dilis down for the night. A storm's coming.'

She welcomed it too. The wind, the rain, the thunder. It stirred something in her, some whippy thrill that made her feel reckless and bold. When Flynn set the fire to blaze with a twist of his hand, her eyes danced.

'I don't suppose you could teach me to do that?'

He glanced back at her, the faintest of smiles, the slightest lift of brow. 'I can't, no. But you've your own magic, Kayleen.'

'Have I?'

'It binds me to you, as I've been bound to no other. I will give you a boon. Any that you ask that is in my power to give.'

'Any?' A smile played around her mouth now as she looked up at him from under her lashes. The blatantly flirtatious move came to her much more naturally than she'd anticipated. 'Well, that's quite an offer. I'll have to consider very carefully before making any decision.'

She wandered the room, trailing a fingertip over the back of the sofa, over the polished gleam of a table. 'Would that offer include, say, the sun and the moon?'

Look at her, he thought. She grows more beautiful by the hour. 'Such as these?' He held out his hands. From them dripped a string of luminous white pearls with a clasp of diamonds.

She laughed, even as her breath caught. 'Those aren't bad, as an example. They're magnificent, Flynn. But I didn't ask for diamonds or pearls.'

'Then I give them freely.' He crossed to her, laid the necklace over her head. 'For the pleasure of seeing you wear them.'

'I've never worn pearls.' Surprised by the delight they brought her, she lifted them, let them run like moonbeams through her fingers. 'They make me feel regal.'

Holding them out, she turned a circle while the diamond clasp exploded with light. 'Where do they come from? Do you just picture them in your mind and ... poof?'

'Poof?' He decided she hadn't meant that as an insult. 'More or less, I suppose. They exist, and I move them from one place to another. From there, to here. Whatever is, that has no will, I can bring here, and keep. Nothing with heart or soul can be taken. But the rest ... It's sapphires, I'm thinking, that suit you best.'

As Kayleen blinked, a string of rich black pearls clasped with brilliant sapphires appeared around her neck. 'Oh! I'll never get used to ... Move them?' She looked back at him. 'You mean take them?'

'Mmm.' He turned to pour glasses of wine.

'But . . . ' Catching her bottom lip between her teeth, she looked around the room. The gorgeous antiques, the modern electronics – which she'd noticed ran without electricity, the glamour of Ming vases, the foolishness of pop art.

Almost nothing in the room would have existed when he'd been banished here.

'Flynn, where do all these things come from? Your television set, your piano, the furniture and rugs and art. The food and wine?'

'All manner of places.'

'How does it work?' She took the wine from him. 'I mean, is it like replicating? Do you copy a thing?'

'Perhaps, if I've a mind to. It takes a bit more time and trouble for that process. You have to know the innards, so to speak, and the composition and all matter of scientific business to make it come right. Easier by far just to transport it.'

'But if you just transport it, if you just take it from one place and bring it here, that's stealing.'

'I'm not a thief.' The idea! 'I'm a magician. The laws aren't the same for us.'

Patience was one of her most fundamental virtues. 'Weren't you punished initially because you took something from someone?'

'That was entirely different. I changed a life for another's gain. And I was perhaps a bit . . . rash. Not that it deserved such a harsh sentence.'

'How do you know what lives you've changed by bringing these here?' She held up the pearls. 'Or any of the other things? If you take someone's property, it causes change, doesn't it? And at the core of it, it's just stealing.' Not without regret, she lifted the jewels over her head. 'Now, you have to put these back where you got them.'

'I won't.' Fully insulted now, he slammed his glass down. 'You would reject a gift from me?'

'Yes. If it belongs to someone else. Flynn, I'm a merchant myself. How would I feel to open my shop one morning and find my property gone? It would be devastating. A violation. And beyond that, which is difficult enough, the inconvenience. I'd have to file a police report, an insurance claim. There'd be an investigation, and—'

'Those are problems that don't exist here,' he interrupted. 'You can't apply your ordinary logic to magic. Magic is.'

'Right is, Flynn, and even magic can't negate what's right. These may be heirlooms. They may mean a great deal to someone even beyond their monetary value. I can't accept them.'

She laid the pearls, the glow and the sparkle, on the table.

'You have no knowledge of what governs me.' The air

began to tremble with his anger. 'No right to question what's inside me. Your world hides from mine, century by century, building its pale layers of reason and denial. You come here, and in days you stand in judgment of what you can't begin to comprehend?'

'I don't judge you, Flynn, but your actions.' The wind had come into the room. It blew over her face, through her hair. And it was cold. Though her belly quaked, she lifted her chin. 'Power shouldn't take away human responsibility. It should add to it. I'm surprised you haven't learned that in all the time you've had to think.'

His eyes blazed. He threw out his arms, and the room exploded with sound and light. She stumbled back, but managed to regain her balance, managed to swallow a cry. When the air cleared again, the room was empty but for the two of them.

'This is what I might have if I lived by your rules. Nothing. No comfort, no humanity. Only empty rooms, where even the echoes are lifeless. Five hundred years of alone, and I should worry that another whose life comes and goes in a blink might do without a lamp or a painting?'

'Yes.'

Temper snapped off him, little flames of gold. Then he vanished before her eyes.

What had she done? Panicked, she nearly called out for him, then realized he would hear only what he chose to hear.

She'd driven him away, she thought, sinking down in misery to sit on the bare floor. Driven him away with her rigid stance on right and wrong, her own unbending rules of conduct, just as she had kept so many others at a distance most of her life.

She'd preached at him, she admitted with a sigh. This incredible man with such a magnificent gift. She had wagged her finger at him, just the way she wagged it at her mother. Taken on, as she habitually did, the role of adult to the child.

It seemed that not even magic could burn that irritating trait out of her. Not even love could overcome it.

Now she was alone in an empty room. Alone, as she had been for so long. Flynn thought he had a lock on loneliness, she thought with a half laugh. She'd made a career out of alone.

She drew up her knees, rested her forehead on them. The worst of it, she realized, was that even now – sad, angry, aching – she believed she was right.

It wasn't a hell of a lot of comfort.

7

It took him hours to work off his temper. He walked, he paced, he raged, he brooded. When temper had burned off, he sulked, though if anyone had put this term on his condition, he'd have swung hard back into temper again.

She'd hurt him. When anger cleared away enough for that realization to surface, it came as a shock. The woman had cut him to the bone. She'd rejected his gift, questioned his morality, and criticized his powers. All in one lump.

In his day such a swipe from a mere woman would have . . .

He cursed and paced some more. It wasn't his day, and if there was one thing he'd learned to adjust to, it was the changes in attitudes and sensibilities. Women stood toe-to-toe with men in this age, and in his readings and viewings over the years, he'd come to believe they had the right of it.

He was hardly steeped in the old ways. Hadn't he embraced technology with each new development? Hadn't he amused himself with the quirks of society and fashion and mores as they shifted and changed and became? And he'd taken from each of those shifts what appealed most, what sat best with him.

He was a well-read man, had been well read and well traveled even in his own time. And since that time, he'd studied. Science, history, electronics, engineering, art, music, literature, politics. He had hardly stopped using his mind over the last five hundred years.

The fact was, he rarely had the chance to use anything else.

So, he used it now and went over the argument in his head.

She didn't understand, he decided. Magic wasn't bound by the rules of her world, but by itself. It was, and that was all. No conscientious magician brought harm to another deliberately, that was certain. All he'd done was take a few examples of technology, of art and comfort, from various points in time. He could hardly be expected to live in a bloody cave, could he?

Stealing? Why, the very idea of it!

He sat on a chair in his workshop and indulged in more brooding.

It wasn't meant to be stealing, he thought now. Magicians had moved matter from place to place since the beginning of things. And what were jewels but pretty bits of matter?

Then he sighed. He supposed they were considerably more, from her point of view. And he'd wanted her to see them as more. He'd wanted her to be dazzled and delighted, and dote on him for the gift of them.

Much as he had, he admitted, wanted to dazzle and delight the woman who'd betrayed him. Or, to be honest, the woman who'd tempted him to betray himself and his art. That woman had greedily gathered what he'd given, what he'd taken, and left him to hang.

What had Kayleen done? Had she been overpowered by the glitter and the richness? Seduced by them?

Not in the least. She'd tossed them back in his face.

Stood up for what she believed was right and just.

Stood up to him. His lips began to curve with the image of that. He hadn't expected her to, he could admit that. She'd looked him in the eye, said her piece, and stuck to it.

God, what a woman! His Kayleen was strong and true. Not a bauble to ride on a man's arm but a partner to stand tall with him. That was a grand thing. For while a man might indulge himself in a pretty piece of fluff for a time, it was a woman he wanted for a lifetime.

He got to his feet, studied his workroom. Well, a woman was what he had. He'd best figure out how to make peace with her.

Kayleen considered having a good cry, but it just wasn't like her. She settled instead for hunting up the kitchen which was no easy task. On the search she discovered Flynn had chosen to make his point with only that one empty room. The rest of the house was filled to brimming, and in his fascinatingly eclectic style.

She softened by the time she brewed tea in a kitchen equipped with a restaurant-style refrigerator, a microwave oven, and a stone fireplace in lieu of stove. It took her considerable time to get the fire going and to heat water in the copper pot. But it made her smile.

How could she blame him, really, for wanting things around him? Pretty things, interesting things. He was a man who needed to use his mind, amuse himself, challenge himself. Wasn't that the man she'd fallen in love with?

She carried the tea into the library with its thousands of books, its scrolls, its manuscripts. And its deep-cushioned leather chairs and snappy personal computer.

She would light the fire, and enough candles to read by, then enjoy her tea and the quiet.

Kneeling at the hearth, she tried to light the kindling and managed to scorch the wood. She rearranged the logs, lodged a splinter painfully in her thumb, and tried again.

She created a hesitant little flame, and a great deal of smoke, which the wind cheerfully blew back in her face. She hissed at it, sucked on her throbbing thumb, then sat on her heels to think it through.

And the flames burst into light and heat.

She set her teeth, fought the urge to turn around. 'I can do it myself, thank you.'

'As you wish, lady.'

The fire vanished but for the smoke. She coughed, waved it away from her face, then got to her feet. 'It's warm enough without one.'

'I'd say it's unnaturally chilly at the moment.' He

walked up behind her, took her hand in his. 'You've hurt yourself.'

'It's only a splinter. Don't,' she said when he lifted it to his lips.

'Being strong-minded and being contrary are two different matters.' He touched his lips to her thumb, and the throbbing eased. 'But not contrary enough, I notice, to ignore the comforts of a cup of tea, a book, and a pleasant chair.'

'I wasn't going to stand in an empty room wringing my hands while you worked out your tantrum.'

He lifted his eyebrows. 'Disconcerting, isn't it? Emptiness.'

She tugged her hand free of his. 'All right, yes. And I have no true conception of what you've dealt with, nor any right to criticize how you compensate. But—'

'Right is right,' he finished. 'This place and what I possessed was all I had when first I came here. I could fill it with things, the things that appealed to me. That's what I did. I won't apologize for it.'

'I don't want an apology.'

'No, you want something else entirely.' He opened his hands, and the rich loops of pearls gleamed in them.

'Flynn, don't ask me to take them.'

'I am asking. I give you this gift, Kayleen. They're

replicas, and belong to no one but me. Until they belong to you.'

Her throat closed as he placed them around her neck. 'You made them for me?'

'Perhaps I'd grown a bit lazy over the years. It took me a little longer to conjure them than it might have, but it made me remember the pleasure of making.'

'They're more beautiful than the others. And much more precious.'

'And here's a tear,' he murmured, and caught it on his fingertip as it spilled onto her cheek. 'If it falls from happiness, it will shine. If it's from sorrow, it will turn to ashes. See.'

The drop glimmered on his finger, shimmered, then solidified into a diamond in the shape of a tear. 'And this is your gift to me.' He drew the pendant from beneath his shirt, passed his hand over it. The diamond drop sparkled now beneath the moonstone. 'I'll wear it near my heart. Ever.'

She leapt into his arms, clung to his neck. 'I missed you!'

'I let temper steal hours from us.'

'So did I.' She leaned back. 'We've had our first fight. I'm glad. Now we never have to have a first one again.'

'But others?'

'We'll have to.' She kissed his cheek. 'There's so much we don't understand about each other. And even when we do, we won't always agree.'

'Ah, my sensible Kayleen. No, don't frown,' he said, tipping up her chin. 'I like your mind. It stimulates my own.'

'It annoyed you.'

'At the first of it.' He circled her around, lighting the fire, the candles as he did. 'And I spent a bit of time pondering on how much more comfortable life would be if you'd just be biddable and agree with everything I said and did. "Yes, Flynn, my darling," you would say. "No indeed, my handsome Flynn."'

'Oh, really?'

'But then I'd miss that battle light in your eyes, wouldn't I, and the way your lovely mouth goes firm. Makes me want to . . . ' He nipped her bottom lip. 'But that's another kind of stimulation altogether. I'm willing to fight with you, Kayleen, as long as you're willing to make up again with me.'

'And I'm willing to have you stomp off in a temper—'

'I didn't stomp.'

'Metaphorically speaking. As long as you come back.' She laid her head on his shoulder, closed her eyes. 'The storm's passed,' she murmured. 'Moonlight's shining through the windows.'

'So it is.' He scooped her up. 'I have the perfect way to celebrate our first fight.' He closed her hand over his pendant. 'Would you like to fly, Kayleen?'

'Fly? But—'

And she was soaring through the air, through the night. Air swirled around her, then seemed to go fluid so it was like cutting clean through a dark sea. The stone pulsed against her palm. She cried out in surprise, and then in delight, reaching out as if she could snatch one of the stars that shone around her.

Fearless, Flynn thought, even now, Or perhaps it was more a thirst for all the times she'd denied herself a drink. When she turned her face to his, her eyes brighter than the jewels, brighter than the stars, he spun her in dizzying circles.

They landed in a laughing tumble to roll over the soft cushion of grass by the side of his blue waterfall.

'Oh! That was amazing. Can we do it again?'

'Soon enough. Here.' He lifted a hand, and a plump peach balanced on the tips of his fingers. 'You haven't eaten your supper.'

'I wasn't hungry before.' Charmed, she took the peach,

bit into the sweetness. 'So many stars,' she murmured, lying back again to watch them. 'Were we really flying up there?'

'It's a kind of manipulation of time and space and matter. It's magic. That's enough, isn't it?'

'It's everything. The world's magic now.'

'But you're cold,' he said when she shivered.

'Mmm. Only a little.' Even as she spoke, the air warmed, almost seemed to bloom.

'I confess it.' He leaned over to kiss her. 'I stole a bit of warmth from here and there. But I don't think anyone will miss it. I don't want you chilled.'

'Can it always be like this?'

There was a hitch in his chest. 'It can be what we make it. Do you miss what was before?'

'No.' But she lowered her lashes, so he was unable to read her eyes. 'Do you? I mean, the people you knew? Your family?'

'They've been gone a long time.'

'Was it hard?' She sat up, handed him the peach. 'Knowing you'd never be able to see them again, or talk to them, or even tell them where you were?'

'I don't remember.' But he did. This was the first lie he'd told her. He remembered that the pain of it had been like death.

'I'm sorry.' She touched his shoulder. 'It hurts you.'

'It fades.' He pushed away, got to his feet. 'All of that is beyond, and it fades. It's the illusion, and this is all that's real. All that matters. All that matters is here.'

'Flynn.' She rose, hoping to comfort, but when he spun back, his eyes were hot, bright. And the desire in them robbed her of breath.

'I want you. A hundred lifetimes from now I'll want you. It's enough for me. Is it enough for you?'

'I'm here.' She held out her hands. 'And I love you. It's more than I ever dreamed of having.'

'I can give you more. You still have a boon.'

'Then I'll keep it. Until I need more.' Because he'd yet to take her offered hands, she cupped his face in them. 'I've never touched a man like this. With love and desire. Do you think, Flynn, that because I've never felt them before I don't understand the wonder of knowing them now? Of feeling them now for one man? I've watched my mother search all of her life, be willing to risk heartbreak for the chance – just the chance – of feeling what I do right at this moment. She's the most important person to me outside this world you've made. And I know she'd be thrilled to know what I've found with you.'

'Then when you ask me for your heart's desire, I'll move heaven and earth to give it to you. That's my vow.'

'I have my heart's desire.' She smiled, stepped back. 'Tell me yours.'

'Not tonight. Tonight I have plans for you that don't involve conversation.'

'Oh? And what might they be?'

'Well, to begin ... '

He lifted a hand and traced one finger down through the air between them. Her clothes vanished.

8

'Oh!' this time she instinctively covered herself. 'You might have warned me.'

'I'll have you bathed in moonlight, and dressed in starshine.'

She felt a tug, gentle but insistent, on her hands. Her arms lowered, spread out as if drawn by silken rope. 'Flynn.'

'Let me touch you.' He kept his eyes on hers as he stepped forward, as he traced his fingertips down her throat, over the swell of her breasts. 'Excite you.' He took her mouth in quick, little bites. 'Possess you.'

Something slid through her mind, her body, at the same time. A coiled snake of heat that bound both together. The rise of it, so fast, so sharp, slashed through her. She hadn't the breath to cry out, she could only moan.

He had barely touched her.

'How can you . . . how could I—'

'I want to show you more this time.' Now his hands were on her, rough and insistent. Her skin was so soft, so fragrant. In the moonlight it gleamed so that wherever he touched, the warmth bloomed on it. Roses on silk. 'I want to take more this time.'

For a second time he took her flying. Though her feet never left the ground, she spun through the air. A fast, reckless journey. His mouth was on her, devouring flesh. She had no choice but to let him feed. And his greed erased her past reason so that her one desire was to be consumed.

Abandoning herself to it, she let her head fall back, murmuring his name like a chant as he ravished her.

He mated his mind with hers, thrilling to every soft cry, every throaty whimper. She stood open to him in the moonlight, soaked with pleasure and shuddering from its heat.

And such was his passion for her that his fingers left trails of gold over her damp flesh, trails that pulsed, binding her in tangled ribbons of pleasure.

When his mouth found hers again, the flavor exploded, sharp and sweet. Drunk on her, he lifted them both off the ground.

Now freed, her arms came tight around him, her nails scraping as she sought to hold, sought to find. She was hot against him, wet against him, her hips arching in rising demand.

He drove himself into her, one desperate thrust, then another. Another. With her answering beat for urgent beat, he let the animal inside him spring free.

His mind emptied but for her and that primal hunger they shared. The forest echoed with a call of triumph as that hunger swallowed them both.

She lay limp, useless. Used. A thousand wild horses could have stampeded toward her, and she wouldn't have moved a muscle.

The way Flynn had collapsed on her, and now lay like the dead, she imagined he felt the same.

'I'm so sorry,' she said on a long, long sigh.

'Sorry?' He slid his hand through the grass until it covered hers.

'Umm. So sorry for the women who don't have you for a lover.'

He made a sound that might have been a chuckle. 'Generous of you, *mavourneen*. I prefer being smug that I'm the only man who's had the delights of you.'

'I saw stars. And not the ones up there.'

'So did I. You're the only one who's given me the stars.' He stirred, pressing his lips to the side of her breast before lifting his head. 'And you give me an appetite as well – for all manner of succulent things.'

'I suppose that means you want *your* supper and we have to go back.'

'We have to do nothing but what pleases us. What would you like?'

'At the moment? I'd settle for some water. I've never been so thirsty.'

'Water, is it?' He angled his head, grinned. 'That I can give you, and plenty.' He gathered her up and rolled. She managed a scream, and he a wild laugh, as they tumbled off the bank and hit the water of the pool with a splash.

It seemed miraculous to Kayleen how much she and Flynn had in common. Considering the circumstance and all that differed between them, it was an amazing thing that they found any topic to discuss or explore.

But then, Flynn hadn't sat idle for five hundred years. His

love of something well made, even if its purpose was only for beauty, struck home with her. All of her life she'd been exposed to craftsmanship and aesthetics – the history of a table, the societal purpose of an enameled snuffbox, or the heritage of a serving platter. The few pieces she'd allowed herself to collect were special to her, not only because of their beauty but also because of their continuity.

She and Flynn had enjoyed many of the same books and films, though he had read and viewed far more for the simple enjoyment of it than she.

He listened to her, posing questions about various phases of her life, until she was picking them apart for him and remembering events and things she'd seen or done or experienced that she'd long ago forgotten.

No one had ever been so interested in her before, in who she was and what she thought What she felt. If he didn't agree, he would lure her into a debate or tease her into exploring a lighter side of herself rarely given expression.

It seemed she did the same for him, nudging him out of his brooding silences, or leaving him be until the mood had passed on its own.

But whenever she made a comment or asked a question about the future, those silences lasted long.

So she wouldn't ask, she told herself. She didn't need to

know. What had planning and preciseness gotten her, really, but a life of sameness? Whatever happened when the week was up – God, why couldn't she remember what day it was – she would be content.

For now, every moment was precious.

He'd given her so much. Smiling, she wandered the house, running her fingers along the exquisite pearls, which she hadn't taken off since he'd put them around her neck. Not the gifts, she thought, though she treasured them, but romance, possibilities, and above all, a vision.

She had never seen so clearly before.

Love answered all questions.

What could she give him? Gifts? She had nothing. What little she still possessed was in the car she'd left abandoned in the wood. There was so little there, really, of the woman she'd become, and was still becoming.

She wanted to do something for him. Something that would make him smile.

Food. Delighted with the idea, she hurried back toward the kitchen. She'd never known anyone to appreciate a single bite of apple as much as Flynn.

Of course, since there wasn't any stove, she hadn't a clue what she could prepare, but . . . She swung into the kitchen, stopped short in astonishment.

There certainly was one beauty of a stove now. White and gleaming. All she'd done was mutter about having to boil water for tea over a fire and – poof! – he'd made a stove.

Well, she thought, and pushed up her sleeves, she would see just what she could do with it.

In his workroom, Flynn gazed through one of his windows on the world. He'd intended to focus on Kayleen's home so that he could replicate some of her things for her. He knew what it was to be without what you had, what had mattered to you.

For a time he lost himself there, moving his mind through the rooms where she had once lived, studying the way she'd placed her furniture, what books were on her shelves, what colors she'd favored.

How tidy it all was, he thought with a great surge in his heart. Everything so neatly in place, and so tastefully done. Did it upset her sense of order to be in the midst of his hodgepodge?

He would ask her. They could make some adjustments. But why the hell hadn't the woman had more color around her? And look at the clothes in the closet. All of them more suited to a spinster – no, that wasn't the word used well these days. Plain attire without the richness of fabric and the brilliance of color that so suited his Kayleen.

She would damn well leave them behind if he had any say in it.

But she would want her photographs, and that lovely pier glass there, and that lamp. He began to set them in his mind, the shape and dimensions, the tone and texture. So deep was his concentration that he didn't realize the image had changed until the woman crossed his vision.

She walked through the rooms, her hands clasped tightly together. A lovely woman, he noted. Smaller than Kayleen, fuller at the breasts and hips, but with the same coloring. She wore her dark hair short, and it swung at her cheeks as she moved.

Compelled, he opened the window wider and heard her speak.

'Oh, baby, where are you? Why haven't you called? It's almost a week. Why can't we find you? Oh, Kayleen.' She picked up a photograph from a table, pressed it to her. 'Please be all right. Please be okay.'

With the picture hugged to her heart, she dropped into a chair and began to weep.

Flynn slammed the window shut and turned away.

He would not be moved. He would not.

Time was almost up. In little more than twenty-four hours, the choice would be behind him. Behind them all.

He closed his mind to a mother's grief. But he wasn't fully able to close his heart.

His mood was edgy when he left the workroom. He meant to go outside, to walk it off. Perhaps to whistle up Dilis and ride it off. But he heard her singing.

He'd never heard her sing before. A pretty voice, he thought, but it was the happiness in it that drew him back to the kitchen.

She was stirring something on the stove, something in the big copper kettle that smelled beyond belief.

It had been a very long time since he'd come into a kitchen where cooking was being done. But he was nearly certain that was what had just happened. Since it was almost too marvelous to believe, he decided to make sure of it.

'Kayleen, what are you about there?'

'Oh!' Her spoon clattered, fell out of her hand and plopped into the pot. 'Damn it, Flynn! You startled me. Now look at that, I've drowned the spoon in the sauce.'

'Sauce?'

'I thought I'd make spaghetti. You have a very unusual collection of ingredients in your kitchen. Peanut butter, pickled herring, enough chocolate to make an entire elementary school hyper for a month. However, I managed to find plenty of herbs, and some lovely ripe tomatoes, so this seemed the safest bet. Plus you have ten pounds of spaghetti pasta.'

'Kayleen, are you cooking for me?'

'I know it must seem silly, as you can snap up a five-star meal for yourself without breaking a sweat. But there's something to be said for home cooking. I'm a very good cook. I took lessons. Though I've never attempted to make sauce in quite such a pot, it should be fine.'

'The pot's wrong?'

'Oh, well, I'd do better with my own cookware, but I think I've made do. You had plenty of fresh vegetables in your garden, so I—'

'Just give me a few moments, won't you? I'll need a bit of time.'

And before she could answer, he was gone.

'Well.' She shook her head and went back to trying to save the spoon.

She had everything under control again, had adjusted the heat to keep the sauce at low simmer, when a clatter behind her made her jolt. The spoon plopped back into the sauce.

'Oh, for heaven's sake!' She turned around, then stumbled

back. There was a pile of pots and pans on the counter beside her.

'I replicated them,' Flynn said with a grin. 'Which took me a little longer, but I didn't want to argue with you about it. Then you might not feed me.'

'My pots!' She fell on them with the enthusiasm of a mother for lost children.

More enthusiasm, Flynn realized as she chattered and held up each pan and lid to examine, than she'd shown for the jewels he'd given her.

Because they were hers. Something that belonged to her. Something from her world.

And his heart grew heavy.

'This is going to be good.' She stacked the cookware neatly, selected the proper pot. 'I know it must seem a waste of time and effort to you,' she said as she transferred the sauce. 'But cooking's a kind of art. It's certainly an occupation. I'm used to being busy. A few days of leisure is wonderful, but I'd go crazy after a while with nothing to do. Now I can cook.'

While the sauce simmered in the twenty-first-century pot, she carried the ancient kettle to the sink to wash it. 'And dazzle you with my brilliance,' she added with a quick, laughing glance over her shoulder.

'You already dazzle me.'

'Well, just wait. I was thinking, as I was putting all this together, that I could spend weeks, months, really, organizing around here. Not having a pattern is one thing, but having no order at all is another. You could use a catalogue system for your books. And some of the rooms are just piled with things. I don't imagine you even know what there is. You could use a listing of your art, and the antiques, your music. You have the most extensive collection of antique toys I've ever seen. When we have children . . . '

She trailed off, her hands fumbling in the soapy water. Children. Could they have children? What were the rules? Might she even now be pregnant? They'd done nothing to prevent conception. Or she hadn't, she thought, pressing her lips together.

How could she know what he might have done?

'Listen to me.' She shook her hair back, briskly rinsed the pot. 'Old habits. Lists and plans and procedures. The only plan we need right now is what sort of dressing I should make for the salad.'

'Kayleen.'

'No, no, this is my performance here. You'll just have to find something to do until curtain time.' She heard the sorrow in his voice, the regret. And had her answers. 'Everything should be ready in an hour. So, out.'

She turned, smiling, shooing at him. But her voice was too thick.

'I'll go and tend to Dilis, then.'

'Good, that's fine.'

He left the room, waited. When the tear fell from her eye he brought it from her cheek into his palm. And watched it turn to ashes.

9

He brought her flowers for the table, and they ate her meal with the candles glowing.

He touched her often, just a brush of fingers on the back of her hand. A dozen sensory memories stored for a endless time of longing.

He made her laugh, to hear the sound of it and store that as well. He asked her questions only to hear her voice, the rise and fall of it.

When the meal was done, he walked with her, to see how the moonlight shone in her hair.

Late into the night, he made love with her, as tenderly as he knew how. And knew it was for the last time.

When she slept, when he sent her deep into easy dreams, he was resolved, and he was content with what needed to be done.

She dreamed, but the dreams weren't easy ones. She was lost in the forest, swallowed by the mists that veiled the trees and smothered the path. Light shimmered through it, so drops of moisture glittered like jewels. Jewels that melted away at the touch of her hand, and left her nothing.

She could hear sounds – footsteps, voices, even music – but they seemed to come from underwater. Drowning sounds that never took substance. No matter how hard she tried to find the source, she could come no closer.

The shapes of trees were blurred, the color of the flowers deadened. When she tried to call out, her voice seemed to carry no farther than her own ears.

She began to run, afraid of being lost and being alone. She only had to find the way out. There was always a way out. And her way back to him. As panic gushed inside her, she tried to tear the mists away, ripping at them with her fingers, beating at them with her fists.

But her hands only passed through, and the curtain stayed whole.

Finally, through it, she saw the faint shadow of the house. The spear of its turrets, the sweep of its battlements were softened like wax in the thick air. She ran toward it, sobbing with relief. Then with joy as she saw him standing by the massive doors.

She ran to him now, her arms flung out to embrace, her lips curved for that welcoming kiss.

When her arms passed through him, she understood he was the mist.

And so was she.

She woke weeping and reaching out for him, but the bed beside her was cold and empty. She shivered, though the fire danced cheerfully to warm the room. A dream, just a dream. That was all. But she was cold, and she got out of bed to wrap herself in the thick blue robe.

Where was Flynn? she wondered. They always woke together, almost as if they were tied to each other's rhythms. She glanced out the windows as she walked toward the fire to warm her chilled hands. The sun was beaming and bright, which explained why Flynn hadn't been wrapped around her when she woke.

She'd slept away the morning.

Imagine that, she thought with a laugh. Slept away the morning, dreamed away the night. It was so unlike her.

111

So unlike her, she thought again as her hands stilled. Dreaming. She never remembered her dreams, not even in jumbled pieces. Yet this one she remembered exactly, in every detail, almost as though she'd lived it.

Because she was relaxed, she assured herself. Because her mind was relaxed and open. People were always saying how real dreams could be, weren't they? She'd never believed that until now.

If hers were going to be that frightening, that heart-breaking, she'd just as soon skip them.

But it was over, and it was a beautiful day. There were no mists blanketing the trees. The flowers were basking in the sunlight, their colors vibrant and true. The clouds that so often stacked themselves in layers over the Irish sky had cleared, leaving a deep and brilliant blue.

She would pick flowers and braid them into Dilis's mane. Flynn would give her another riding lesson. Later, perhaps she'd begin on the library. It would be fun to prowl through all the books. To explore them and arrange them.

She would *not* be obsessive about it. She wouldn't fall into that trap again. The chore would be one of pleasure rather than responsibility.

Throwing open the windows, she leaned out, breathed in the sweet air. 'I've changed so much already,' she murmured. 'I like the person I'm becoming. I can be friends with her.'

She shut her eyes tight. 'Mom, I wish I could tell you. I'm so much in love. He makes me so happy. I wish I could let you know, and tell you that I understand now. I wish I could share this with you.'

With a sigh, she stepped back, leaving the windows open.

He kept himself busy. It was the only way he could get through the day. In his mind, in his heart, he'd said goodbye to her the night before. He'd already let her go.

There was no choice but to let her go.

He could have kept her with him, drawing her into the long days, the endless nights of the next dreaming. His solitude would be broken, the loneliness diminished. And at the end of it, she would be there for that brief week. To touch. To be.

The need for her, the desire to have her close, was the strongest force he'd ever known. But for one.

Love.

Not just with the silken beauty of the dreams he'd shared with her. But with the pains and joys that came from a beating heart.

He would not deny her life, steal from her what she had known, what she would be. How had he ever believed he could? Had he really thought that his own needs, the most selfish and self-serving of them, outweighed the most basic of hers?

To live. To feel heat and cold, hunger, thirst, pleasure and pain.

To watch herself change with the years. To shake the hand of a stranger, embrace a loved one. To make children and watch them grow.

For all his power, all his knowledge, he could give her none of those things. All he had left for her was the gift of freedom.

To comfort himself, he pressed his face to Dilis's neck, drew in the scents of horse and straw, of oat and leather. How was it he could forget, each time forget the wrenching misery of these last hours? The sheer physical pain of knowing it was all ending again.

He was ending again.

'You've always been free. You know I have no claim to keep you here, should you choose to go.' He lifted his head, stroking the stallion's head as he looked into his eyes. 'Carry her away safe for me. And if you go beyond, I'll not count it against you.'

He stepped back, drew his breath. There was work yet, and the morning was passing fast.

When it was done, the last spell, the thin blanket of forget spread at the edges of his prison, he saw Kayleen in his mind's eye.

She wandered through the gardens toward the verge of the forest. Looking for him, calling his name. The pain was like an arrow in the heart, almost driving him to his knees.

So, he was not prepared after all. He fisted his hands, struggled for composure. Resolved but not prepared. How would he ever live without her?

'She will live without me,' he said aloud. 'That I want more. We'll end it now, quick and clean.'

He could not will her away, will her back into her world and into life. But he could drive her from him, so that the choice to go was her own.

Taking Dilis's reins, only for the comfort of contact, he walked for the last time as a man, for yet a century to come, through the woods toward home.

She heard the jingle of harness and the soft hoofbeats. Relieved, she turned toward the sound, walking quickly as Flynn came out of the trees.

'I wondered where you were.' She threw her arms around his neck, and he let her. Her mouth pressed cheerfully to his, and he absorbed the taste of it.

'Oh, I had a bit of work.' The words cut at his throat like shards of glass. 'It's a fine day for it, and for your travels.'

'For my travels.'

'Indeed.' He gave her a little pat, then moved away to adjust the stirrups of Dilis's saddle. 'I've cleared the path, so you'll have no trouble. You'll find your way easily enough. You're a resourceful woman.'

'My way? Where?'

He glanced back, gave her an absent smile. 'Out, of course. It's time for you to go.'

'Go?'

'There, that should do.' He turned to her fully. Every ounce of power he owned went into the effort. 'Dilis will take you as far as you need. I'd go with you myself, but I've so much to see to yet. I saw you have one of those little pocket phones in your car. Fascinating things, I have to remember to get one myself for the study of it. You should be able to use it once you're over the border.'

'I don't understand what you're saying.' How could she when her mind had gone numb, when her heart had stopped beating. 'I'm not going.'

'Kayleen, darling, of course you are.' He patted her cheek. 'Not that it hasn't been a delight having you here. I don't know when I've been so diverted.'

'Di . . . *diverted*?'

'Mmm. God, you're a tasty bit,' he murmured, then leaned down to nip at her bottom lip. 'Perhaps we could take just enough time to . . . ' His hands roamed down her, giving her breasts a teasing squeeze.

'Stop!' She stumbled back, came up hard against Dilis, who shifted, restless. 'A diversion? That's all this was to you? A way to pass the time?'

'Passed it well, didn't we? Ah, sweetheart, I gave as much pleasure as I got. You can't deny it. But we've both got things to get back to, don't we?'

'I love you.'

She was killing him. 'God bless the female heart.' And he said it with a chuckle. 'It's so generous.' Then he lifted his brows, rolled his eyes under them. 'Ah, don't be making a scene and spoil this parting moment. We've enjoyed each other, and that's the end. Where did you think this was going? It's time out of time, Kayleen. Now don't be stubborn.'

'You don't love me. You don't want me.'

'I loved you well enough.' He winked at her. 'And wanted you plenty.' When the tears swam into her eyes, he threw up his hands as if exasperated. 'For pity's sake, woman, I brought some magic and romance into a life you yourself

117

said was tedious. I gave you some sparkle.' He lifted her pearls with a fingertip.

'I never asked for jewels. I never wanted anything but you.'

'Took them, though, didn't you? Just as another took the sparkles from me once. Do you think, after having a woman damn me to this place, I'd want another around for longer than it takes to amuse myself?'

'I'm not like her. You can't believe—'

'A woman's a woman,' he said carelessly. 'And I've given you a pretty holiday, with souvenirs besides. The least you can do is be grateful and go along when I bid you. I've no more time for you, and none of the patience to dry your tears and cuddle. Up you go.'

He lifted her, all but tossed her into the saddle.

'You said you wouldn't hurt me.' She dragged the pearls over her head, hurled them into the dirt at his feet. She stared at him, and in his face she saw the savageness again, the brutality, and none of the tenderness. 'You lied.'

'You hurt yourself, by believing what wasn't there. Go back to your tame world. You've no place in mine.'

He slapped a hand violently on Dilis's flank. The horse reared, then lunged forward.

When she was gone, swallowed up by the forest, Flynn dropped to his knees on the ground – and grieved.

10

She wanted to find anger. Bitterness. Anything that would overpower this hideous pain. It had dried up even her tears, had smothered any rage or sorrow before it could fully form.

It had all been a lie. Magic was nothing but deceit.

In the end, love hadn't been the answer. Love had done nothing but make her a fool.

Didn't it prove she'd been right all along? Her disdain of the happy ending her mother had regaled her with had been sense, not stubbornness. There were no fairy tales, no loves that conquered all, no grand sweep of romance to ride on forever.

Letting herself believe, even for a little while, had shattered her.

Yet how could she not have believed? Wasn't she even now riding on a white horse through the forest? That couldn't be denied. If she'd misplaced her heart, she couldn't deny all that she'd seen and done and experienced. How did she, logical Kayleen, resolve the unhappy one with the magnificent other?

How could he have given her so much, shown her so much, and thought of her as only a kind of temporary entertainment? No, no, something was wrong. Why couldn't she think?

Dilis walked patiently through the trees as she pondered. It had all happened so quickly. This change in him had come like a fingersnap, and left her reeling and helpless. Now, she willed her mind to clear, to analyze. But after only moments, her thoughts became scattered and jumbled once again.

Her car was unmarked, shining in the sunlight that dappled through the trees. It sat tidily on a narrow path that ran straight as a ruler through the forest.

He'd cleared the path, he'd said. Well, he certainly was a man of his word. She slid off the horse, slowly circled the car. Not a scratch, she noted. Considerate of him. She wouldn't have to face the hassle that a wrecked car would have caused with the rental company.

Yes, he'd cleared that path as well. But why had he bothered with such a mundane practicality?

Curious, she opened the car door and sliding behind the wheel, turned the key. The engine sprang to life, purred.

Runs better than it did when I picked it up, she thought. And look at that, to top things off, we have a full tank.

'Did you want me out of your life so badly, Flynn, that you covered all contingencies? Why were you so cruel at the end? Why did you work so hard to make me hate you?'

He'd given her no reason to stay, and every rational reason to go.

With a sigh, she got out of the car to say good-bye to Dilis. She indulged herself, running her hands over his smooth hide, nuzzling at his throat. Then she patted his flank. 'Go back to him now,' she murmured, and turned away to spare her heart as the horse pranced off.

Because she wanted some tangible reminder of her time there, she picked a small nosegay of wildflowers, twined the stems together, and regardless of the foolishness of the gesture, tucked them into her hair.

She got into the car again and began to drive.

The sun slanted in thin beams through the trees, angled over the little lane. As she glanced in her mirror, she saw the path shimmer, then vanish behind her in a tumble of moss and stones and brambles. Soon there would be nothing but the silent wood, and no trace that she had ever walked there with a lover.

But she would remember, always, the way he'd looked at her, the way he would press his lips to the heart of her hand. The way he'd bring her flowers and scatter them over her hair.

The way his eyes would warm with laughter, or heat with passion when ... His eyes. What color were his eyes? Slightly dizzy, she stopped the car, pressed her fingers to her temples.

She couldn't bring his face into her mind, not clearly. How could she not know the color of his eyes? Why couldn't she quite remember the sound of his voice?

She shoved out of the car, stumbled a few steps. What was happening to her? She'd been driving from Dublin on the way to her bed-and-breakfast. A wrong turn. A storm. But what ...

Without thinking, she took another step back down the now overgrown path. And her mind snapped clear as crystal.

Her breath was coming short. She turned, stared at the car, the clear path in front of it, the impassable ground behind.

'Flynn's eyes are green,' she said. His face came clearly into her mind now. And when she took a cautious step forward, her memory of him went hazy.

This time she stepped back quickly, well back. 'You wanted me to forget you. Why? Why if none of it mattered did you care if I remembered you or not? Why would it matter if I broke my heart over you?'

A little shaky, she sat down on the ground. And she began to do what she'd always done best. Be logical.

Flynn sat as he had on the night it had begun. In the chair in front of the fire in the tower. He'd watched in the flames until Kayleen had gotten into her car. After that, he hadn't been able to bear it, so he had hazed the vision with smoke.

He'd lost track of the time that he'd sat there now, chained by his own grief. He knew the day was passing. The slant of sunlight through the window had shortened and was dimming.

She would be beyond now, and would have forgotten him. That was for the best. There would be some confusion, of course. A loss of time never fully explained. But she would put that behind her as well.

In a year or two, or twenty, he might look into the fire again, and see how she was. But he would never open his mind to her in dreams, for that would be more torment than he could ever possibly bear.

She would be changed a little by what had passed between them. More open to possibilities, to the magic of life. He lifted the strings of pearls, watched them glow in the light of the dying fire. At least that was a gift she hadn't been able to hurl at his feet.

With the pearls wrapped around his fingers, he lowered his face into his hands. He willed the time to come when pain could strike only his mind, when every sense wasn't tuned so sharply that he could smell her even now. That soft scent that whispered in the air.

'Bring on the bloody night,' he muttered and threw his head back.

Then he was stumbling to his feet, staring. She stood not three feet away. Her hair was tangled, her clothes torn. Scratches scored her hands and face.

'What trick is this?'

'I want my boon. I want what you promised me.'

'What have you done?' His knees unlocked and he lunged toward her, grabbing her hard by the arms. 'How are you hurt? Look at you. Your hands are all torn and bleeding.'

'You put briars in my way.' She gave him a shove, and such was his shock that she knocked him back two full steps. 'You bastard. It took hours to get through them.'

'Get through.' His head snapped back, as if she'd slapped him. 'You have to go. Go! Now! What's the time?' He was pushing her out of the room, and when that wasn't quick enough he began to drag her.

'I'm not going. Not until you grant my boon.'

'You damn well are.' Terrified, he tossed her over his shoulder and began to run. As she struggled and cursed him, he began to fly.

The night was closing in. Time that had dripped began to flood. He went as deep into the forest as he dared. The edges of his prison seemed to hiss around him.

'There.' Fear for her slicked his skin. 'Your car's just up ahead. Get in it and go.'

'Why? So I can drive a little farther and forget all this? Forget you? You'd have stolen that from me.'

'I've no time to argue with you.' He grabbed her

125

shoulders and shook. 'There is no time. If you stay past the last stroke of twelve, you're trapped here. A hundred years will pass before you can walk away again.'

'Why do you care? It's a big house. A big forest. I won't get in your way.'

'You don't understand. Go. This place is mine, and I don't want you here.'

'You're trembling, Flynn. What frightens you?'

'I'm not frightened, I'm angry. You've abused my hospitality. You're trespassing.'

'Call the cops,' she suggested. 'Call your Keepers. Or . . . why don't you just flick me out, the way you flick things in? But you can't, can you?'

'If I could, you'd be gone already.' He yanked her a few steps toward the car, then swore when the ground in front of his boots began to spark and smoke. That was the edge of his prison.

'Big, powerful magician, but you can't get rid of me that way. You couldn't bring me here, and you can't send me away. Not with magic, because I have heart and soul. I have will. So you tried to drive me away with careless words. Cruel, careless words. You didn't think I'd see through them, did you? Didn't think I'd figure it all out. You forgot who you were dealing with.'

'Kayleen.' He took her hands now, squeezing desperately. 'Do this thing I ask now, won't you?'

'A diversion,' she said. 'That's a crock. You love me.'

'Of course I love you.' He shook her harder, shouted so his voice boomed through the forest. 'That's the bloody point. And if you care for me, you'll do what I tell you, and do it now.'

'You love me.' Her breath came out on a sob as she flung herself against him. 'I knew it. Oh, I'm so angry with you. I'm so in love with you.'

His arms ached to grip, to hold. He made himself push her away, hold her at arm's length. 'Listen to me, Kayleen. Clear the stars out of your eyes and be sensible. I've no right to love you. Be quiet!' he snapped when she started to speak. 'You remember what I told you about this place, about me. Do you feel my hands on you, Kayleen?'

'Yes. They're trembling.'

'After midnight, one breath after, you won't feel them, or anything else. No touch, no contact. You'll pick a flower, but you won't feel the stem or the petals. Its perfume will be lost to you. Can you feel your own heart beat? Beating inside you? You won't. It's worse than death to be and yet not be. Day by day into the decades with nothing of substance. Nothing but what's in your mind. And, *a ghra*, you haven't

127

even the magic to amuse yourself into some sanity. You'll be lost, little more than a ghost.'

'I know.' Like the dream, she thought. A mist within the mist.

'There's more. There can be no children. During the dreaming nothing can grow in you. Nothing can change in or of you. You will have no family, no comfort. No choice. This is my banishment. It will not be yours.'

Though her nerves began to dance, her gaze stayed steady. 'I'll have my boon.'

He swore, threw up his hands. 'Woman, you try me to the bone. All right, then. What will you?'

'To stay.'

'No.'

'You took a vow.'

'And so I break it. What more can be done to me?'

'I'll stay anyway. You can't stop me.'

But he could. There was one way to save her in the time left him. One final way. 'You defeat me.' He drew her close, rocked her against him. 'You've a head like a rock. I love you, Kayleen. I loved you in dreams, when dreams were all there was for me. I love you now. It killed me to hurt you.'

'I want to be with you, no matter how short the time or

how long. We'll dream together until we can live together again.'

He took her mouth. A deep kiss, a drugging one that spun in her head, blurred her vision. Joy settled sweetly in her heart.

When she sighed, he stepped back from her. 'Five hundred years,' he said quietly. 'And only once have I loved. Only you.'

'Flynn.' She started to move toward him, but the air between them had hardened into a shield. 'What is this?' She lifted her fisted hands to it, pushed. 'What have you done?'

'There's a choice, and it's mine to make. I will not damn you to my prison, Kayleen. No power can sway me.

'I won't go.' She pounded a fist on the shield.

'I know it, and understand it as well. I should have before. I would never leave you, either. *Manim astheee hu.*' My soul, he said in the language of his birth, is within you. 'You brought me a gift, Kayleen. Love freely given.'

The wind began to kick. From somewhere a sound boomed, slow and dull, like a clock striking the hour.

'I give you a gift in return. Life to be lived. I have a choice, one offered me long ago. A hundred years times five.'

'What are you . . . No!' She flung herself at the shield, beat against it. 'No, you can't. You'll die. You're five hundred years old. You can't live without your powers.'

'It's my right. My choice.'

'Don't do this.' How many strikes of the clock had there been? 'I'll go. I swear it.'

'There's no time now. My powers,' he said, lifting his arms. 'My blood, my life. For hers.' Lightning spewed from the sky, struck like a comet between them. 'For foolishness, for pride, for arrogance I abjure my gifts, my skills, my birthright. And for love I cast them away.'

His eyes met Kayleen's through the wind and light as the clock struck. 'For love, I offer them freely. Let her forget, for there is no need for her to suffer.'

He fisted his hands, crossed his arms over his chest. Braced as the world went mad around him. 'Now.'

And the clock struck twelve.

The world went still. Overhead the skies broke clear so the stars poured free. The trees stood as if carved out of the dark. The only sound was of Kayleen's weeping.

'Do I dream?' Flynn whispered. Cautious, he held out a hand, opened and closed his fist. Felt the movement of his own fingers.

The air began to stir, a soft, sweet breeze. An owl called.

'I am.' Flynn dropped to his knees beside Kayleen, with wonder in his eyes. 'I am.'

'Flynn!' She threw her arms around him, dragging him close, breathing him in. 'You're real. You're alive.'

'I am restored.' He dropped his head on her shoulder. 'I am freed. The Keepers.'

He was breathless, fighting to clear his mind. Drawing her back, he framed her face in his hands. Solid, warm. His.

'You're free.' She pressed her hands against his. The tears that fell from her eyes shimmered into diamonds on the ground between them. 'You're alive! You're here.'

'The Keepers said I have atoned. I was given love, and I put the one I loved before myself. Love.' He pressed his lips to her brow. 'They told me it is the simplest, and most potent of magic. I took a very long time to learn it.'

'So have I. We saved each other, didn't we?'

'We loved each other. *Manim astheee hu*,' he said again. 'These are the words I give you.' He opened his hand and held out the pearls. 'Will you take them, and this gift, as a symbol of betrothal? Will you take them, and me?'

'I will.'

He drew her to her feet. 'Soon, then, for I've a great respect for time, and the wasting of it. Now, look what you've done.' He trailed his fingers gently over the scratch on her cheek. 'There's a mess you've made of yourself.'

'That's not very romantic.'

'I'll fill you with romance, but first I'll tend those hurts.' He scooped her off her feet.

'My mother's going to be crazy about you.'

'I'm counting on it.' Because he wanted to savor, he walked for a bit. 'Will I like Boston, do you think?'

'Yes, I think you will.' She twirled a lock of his hair around her fingers. 'I could use someone who knows something about antiques in my family business.'

'Is that so? Ha. A job. Imagine that. I might consider that, if there was thought of opening a branch here in Ireland, where a certain wildly-in-love married couple could split their time, so to speak.'

'I wouldn't have it any other way.'

She laughed as he spun her around, pressed her lips to his, and held on tight as they leaped into space and flew toward home.

And happily-ever-afters.

WINTER ROSE

1

The world was white. And bitter, bitter cold. Exhausted, he drooped in the saddle, unable to do more than trust his horse to continue to trudge forward. Always forward. He knew that to stop, even for moments, in this cruel and keening wind would mean death.

The pain in his side was a freezing burn, and the only thing that kept him from sliding into oblivion.

He was lost in that white globe, blinded by the endless miles of it that covered hill and tree and sky, trapped in the

135

frigid hell of vicious snow gone to icy shards in the whip of the gale. Though even the slow, monotonous movements of his horse brought him agony, he did not yield.

At first the cold had been a relief from the scorching yellow sun. It had, he thought, cooled the fever the wound had sent raging through him. The unblemished stretch of white had numbed his mind so that he'd no longer seen the blood staining the battleground. Or smelled the stench of death.

For a time, when the strength had drained out of him along with his blood, he'd thought he heard voices in the rising wind. Voices that had murmured his name, had whispered another.

Delirium, he'd told himself. For he didn't believe the air could speak.

He'd lost track of how long he'd been traveling. Hours, days, weeks. His first hope had been to come across a cottage, a village where he could rest and have his wound treated. Now he simply wanted to find a decent place to die.

Perhaps he was dead already and hell was endless winter.

He no longer hungered, though the last time he'd eaten had been before the battle. The battle, he thought dimly, where he'd emerged victorious and unscathed. It had been foolish, carelessly foolish, of him to ride for home alone.

The trio of enemy soldiers had, he was sure, been trying to reach their own homes when they met him on that path in the forest. His first instinct was to let them go. The battle had been won and the invasion crushed. But war and death were still in their eyes, and when they charged him his sword was in his hand.

They would never see home now. Nor, he feared, would he.

As his mount plodded onward, he fought to remain conscious. And now he was in another forest, he thought dully as he struggled to focus. Though how he had come to it, how he had gotten lost when he knew his kingdom as intimately as a man knew a lover's face, was a mystery to him.

He had never traveled here before. The trees looked dead to him, brittle and gray. He heard no bird, no brook, just the steady swish of his horse's hooves in the snow.

Surely this was the land of the dead, or the dying.

When he saw the deer, it took several moments to register. It was the first living thing he'd seen since the flakes had begun to fall, and it watched him without fear.

Why not? he mused with a weak laugh. He hadn't the

strength to notch an arrow. When the stag bounded away, Kylar of Mrydon, prince and warrior, slumped over the neck of his horse.

When he came to again, the forest was at his back, and he faced a white, white sea. Or so it seemed. Just as it seemed, in the center of that sea, a silver island glittered. Through his hazy vision, he made out turrets and towers. On the topmost a flag flew in the wild wind. A red rose blooming full against a field of white.

He prayed for strength. Surely where there was a flag flying there were people. There was warmth. He would have given half a kingdom to spend the last hour of his life by a fire's light and heat.

But his vision began to go dark at the edges and his head swam. Through the waves of fatigue and weakness he thought he saw the rose, red as blood, moving over that white sea toward him. Gritting his teeth, he urged his horse forward. If he couldn't have the fire, he wanted the sweet scent of the rose before he died.

He lacked even the strength to curse fate as he slid once more into unconsciousness and tumbled from the saddle into the snow.

The fall shot pain through him, pushed him back to the surface, where he clung as if under a thin veil of ice.

Through it, he saw a face leaning close to his. Lovely long-lidded eyes, green as the moss in the forests of his home, smooth skin of rose and cream. A soft, full mouth. He saw those pretty lips move, but couldn't hear the words she spoke through the buzzing in his head.

The hood of her red cloak covered her hair, and he reached up to touch the cloth. 'You're not a flower after all.'

'No, my lord. Only a woman.'

'Well, it's better to die warmed by a kiss than a fire.' He tugged on the hood, felt that soft, full mouth meet his – one sweet taste – before he passed out.

Men, Deirdre thought as she eased back, were such odd creatures. To steal a kiss at such a time was surely beyond folly. Shaking her head, she got to her feet and took in hand the horn that hung from the sash at her waist. She blew the signal for help, then removed her cloak to spread over him. Sitting again, she cradled him as best she could in her arms and waited for stronger hands to carry the unexpected guest into the castle.

The cold had saved his life, but the fever might snatch it back again. On his side of the battle were his youth and his strength. And, Deirdre thought, herself. She would do all in her power to heal him. Twice, he'd regained consciousness during his transport to the bedchamber. And both times he'd struggled, weakly to be sure, but enough to start the blood flowing from his wound again once he was warm.

In her brisk, somewhat ruthless way, she'd ordered two of her men to hold him down while she doused him with a sleeping draught. The cleaning and closing of the wound would be painful for him if he should wake again. Deirdre was a woman who brooked no nonsense, but she disliked seeing anyone in pain.

She gathered her medicines and herbs, pushed up the sleeves of the rough tunic she wore. He lay naked on the bed, in the thin light of the pale gold sun that filtered through the narrow windows. She'd seen unclothed men before, just as she'd seen what a sword could do to flesh.

'He's so handsome.' Cordelia, the servant Deirdre had ordered to assist her, nearly sighed.

'What he is, is dying.' Deirdre's voice was sharp with command. 'Put more pressure on that cloth. I'll not have him bleed to death under my roof.'

She selected her medicines and, moving to the bed, concentrated only on the wound in his side. It ranged from an inch under his armpit down to his hip in one long, vicious slice. Sweat dewed on her brow as she focused, putting her mind into his body to search for damage. Her cheeks paled as she worked, but her hands were steady and quick.

So much blood, she thought as her breath came thick and ragged. So much pain. How could he have lived with this? Even with the cold slowing the flow of blood, he should have been long dead.

She paused once to rinse the blood from her hands in a bowl, to dry them. But when she picked up the needle, Cordelia blanched. 'My lady . . . '

Absently, Deirdre glanced over. She'd nearly forgotten the girl was there. 'You may go. You did well enough.'

Cordelia fled the room so quickly, Deirdre might have smiled. The girl never moved so fast when there was work to be done. Deirdre turned back to her patient and began carefully, skillfully, to sew the wound closed.

It would scar, she thought, but he had others. His was a warrior's body, tough and hard and bearing the marks of battle. What was it, she wondered, that made men so eager to fight, to kill? What was it that lived inside them that they could find pride in both?

This one did, she was sure of it. It had taken strength and will, and pride, to keep him mounted and alive all the miles he'd traveled to her island. But how had he come, this dark warrior? And why?

She coated the stitched wound with a balm of her own making and bandaged it with her own hands. Then with the worst tended, she examined his body thoroughly for any lesser wounds.

She found a few nicks and cuts, and one more serious slice on the back of his shoulder. It had closed on its own and was already scabbed over. Whatever battle he'd fought, she calculated, had been two days ago, perhaps three.

To survive so long with such grievous hurts, to have traveled through the Forgotten to reach help, showed a strong will to live. That was good. He would need it.

When she was satisfied, she took a clean cloth and began to wash and cool the fever sweat from his skin.

He was handsome. She let herself study him now. He was tall, leanly muscled. His hair, black as midnight, spilled over the bed linens, away from a face that might have been carved from stone. It suited the warrior, she thought, that narrow face with the sharp jut of cheekbones over hollowed cheeks. His nose was long and straight, his mouth full and somewhat hard. His beard had begun to grow in, a shadow of stubble that made him appear wicked and dangerous even unconscious.

His brows were black slashes. She remembered his eyes were blue. Even dazed with pain, fever, fatigue, they had been bold and brilliantly blue.

If the gods willed it, they would open again.

She tucked him up warm, laid another log on the fire. Then she sat down to watch over him.

For two days and two nights the fever raged in him. At times he was delirious and had to be restrained lest his thrashing break open his wound again. At times he slept like a man dead, and she feared he would never rouse. Even her gifts couldn't beat back the fire that burned in him.

She slept when she could in the chair beside his bed. And once, when the chills racked him, she crawled under the bedclothes with him to soothe him with her own body.

His eyes did open again, but they were blind and wild. The pity she tried to hold back when healing stirred inside her. Once, when the night was dark and the cold rattled its bones against the windows, she held his hand and grieved for him.

Life was the most precious gift, and it seemed cruel that he should come so far from home only to lose his.

To busy her mind she sewed or she sang. When she trusted him to be quiet for a time, she left him in the care of one of her women and tended to the business of her home and her people.

On the last night of his fever, despair nearly broke her. Exhausted, she mourned for his wife, for his mother, for those he'd left behind who would never know of his fate. There in the quiet of the bedchamber, she used the last of her strength and her skill. She laid hands on him.

'The first and most vital of rules is not to harm. I have not harmed you. What I do now will end this, one way or another. Kill or cure. If I knew your name' – she brushed a hand gently over his burning brow – 'or your mind, or your heart, this would be easier for both of us. Be strong.' She climbed onto the bed to kneel beside him. 'And fight.'

With one hand over the wound that she'd unbandaged, the other over his heart, she let what she was rush through her, race through her blood, her bone. Into him.

He moaned. She ignored it. It would hurt, hurt both of them. His body arched up, and hers back. There was a rush of images that stole her breath. A grand castle, blurring colors, a jeweled crown.

She felt strength – his. And kindness. A light flickered inside her, nearly made her break away. But it drew her in, deeper, and the light grew soft, warm.

For Deirdre, it was the first time, even in healing that she had looked into another's heart and felt it brush and call her own.

Then she saw, very clearly, a woman's face, her deep-blue eyes full of pride, and perhaps fear.

Come back, my son. Come home safe.

There was music – drumbeats – the laughter and shouts of men. Then a flash that was sun striking off steel, and the smell of blood and battle choked her.

She muffled a cry as she caught a glimpse in her mind. Swords clashing, the stench of sweat and death and fear.

He fought her, thrashing, striking out as she bore down with her mind. Later, she would tend the bruises they gave each other in this final pitched battle for life.

Her muscles trembled, and part of her screamed to pull back, pull away. He was nothing to her. Still, as her muscles trembled, she pit her fire against the fever, just as the enemy sword in his mind slashed against them both.

She felt the bite of it in her side, steel into flesh. The agony ripped a scream from her throat. On its heels, she tasted death.

His heart galloped under her hand, and the wound on his side was like a flame against her palm. But she'd seen into his mind now, and she fought to rise above the pain and use what she'd been given, what she'd taken, to save him.

His eyes were open, glassy with shock in a face white as death.

'Kylar of Mrydon.' She spoke clearly, though each breath she took was a misery. 'Take what you need. Fire of healing. And live.'

The tension went out of his body. His eyes blurred, then fluttered shut. She felt the sigh shudder through him as he slid into sleep.

But the light within her continued to glow. 'What is this?' she murmured, rubbing an unsteady hand over her own heart. 'No matter. No matter now. I can do no more to help you. Live,' she said again, then leaned down to brush her lips over his brow. 'Or die gently.'

She started to climb down from the bed, but her head spun. When she fainted, her head came to rest, quite naturally, on his heart.

2

He drifted in and out. There were times when he thought himself back in battle, shouting commands to his men while his horse wheeled under him and his sword hacked through those who would dare invade his lands.

Then he was back in that strange and icy forest, so cold he feared his bones would shatter. Then the cold turned to fire, and the part of him that was still sane prayed to die.

Something cool and sweet would slide down his throat, and somehow he would sleep again.

He dreamed he was home, drifting toward morning with a willing woman in his bed. Soft and warm and smelling of summer roses.

He thought he heard music, harpsong, with a voice, low and smooth, matching pretty words to those plucked notes.

Sometimes he saw a face. Moss-green eyes, a lovely, wide mouth. Hair the color of dark, rich honey that tumbled around a face both unbearably beautiful and unbearably sad. Each time the pain or the heat or the cold would become intolerable, that face, those eyes, would be there.

Once, he dreamed she had called him by name, in a voice that rang with command. And those eyes had been dark and full of pain and power. Her hair had spilled over his chest like silk, and he'd slept once more – deeply, peacefully – with the scent of her surrounding him.

He woke again to that scent, drifted into it as a man might drift into a cool stream on a hot day. There was a velvet canopy of deep purple over his head. He stared at it as he tried to clear his mind. One thought came through.

This was not home.

Then another.

He was alive.

Morning, he decided. The light through the windows

was thin and very dull. Not long past dawn. He tried to sit up, and the movement made his side throb. Even as he hissed out a breath, she was there.

'Carefully.' Deirdre slid a hand behind his head to lift it gently as she brought a cup to his lips. 'Drink now.'

She gave him no choice but to swallow before he managed to bring his hand to hers and nudge the cup aside. 'What ... ' His voice felt rusty, as if it would scrape his throat. 'What is this place?'

'Drink your broth, Prince Kylar. You're very weak.'

He would have argued, but to his frustration he was as weak as she said. And she was not. Her hands were strong, hard from labor. He studied her as she urged more broth on him.

That honey hair fell straight as rain to the waist of a simple gray dress. She wore no jewels, no ribbons, and still managed to look beautiful and wonderfully female.

A servant, he assumed, with some skill in healing. He would find a way to repay her, and her master.

'Your name, sweetheart?'

Odd creatures indeed, she thought as she arched a brow. A man would flirt the moment he regained what passed for his senses. 'I am Deirdre.'

'I'm grateful, Deirdre. Would you help me up?'

149

'No, my lord. Tomorrow, perhaps.' She set the cup aside. 'But you could sit up for a time while I tend your wound.'

'I dreamed of you.' Weak, yes, he thought. But he was feeling considerably better. Well enough to put some effort into flirting with a beautiful housemaid. 'Did you sing to me?'

'I sang to pass the time. You've been here three days.'

'Three——' He gritted his teeth as she helped him to sit up. 'I've no memory of it.'

'That's natural. Be still now.'

He frowned at her bent head as she removed the bandage. Though a generous man by nature, he wasn't accustomed to taking orders. Certainly not from housemaids. 'I would like to thank your master for his hospitality.'

'There is no master here. It heals clean,' she murmured, and probed gently with her fingers. 'And is cool. You'll have a fine scar to add to your collection.' With quick competence, she smeared on a balm. 'There's pain yet, I know. But if you can tolerate it for now, I'd prefer not to give you another sleeping draught.'

'Apparently I've slept enough.'

She began to bandage him again, her body moving into his as she wrapped the wound. Fetching little thing, he mused, relieved that he was well enough to feel a tug of interest. He skimmed a hand through her hair as she worked, twined a lock around his finger. 'I've never had a prettier physician.'

'Save your strength, my lord.' Her voice was cool, dismissive, and made him frown again. 'I won't see my work undone because you've a yen for a snuggle.'

She stepped back, eyeing him calmly. 'But if you've that much energy, you may be able to take some more broth, and a bit of bread.'

'I'd rather meat.'

'I'm sure. But you won't get it. Do you read, Kylar of Mrydon?'

'Yes, of course I ... You call me by name,' he said cautiously. 'How do you know it?'

She thought of that dip she'd taken into his mind. What she'd seen. What she'd felt. Neither of them, she was sure, was prepared to discuss it. 'You told me a great many things during the fever,' she said. And that was true enough. 'I'll see you have books. Bed rest is tedious. Reading will help.'

She picked up the empty cup of broth and started across the chamber to the door.

'Wait. What is this place?'

She turned back. 'This is Rose Castle, on the Isle of Winter in the Sea of Ice.'

His heart stuttered in his chest, but he kept his gaze direct on hers. 'That's a fairy tale. A myth.'

'It's as real as life, and as death. You, my lord Kylar, are the first to pass this way in more than twenty years. When you're rested and well, we'll discuss how you came here.'

'Wait.' He lifted a hand as she opened the thick carved door. 'You're not a servant.' He wondered how he could ever have mistaken her for one. The simple dress, the lack of jewels, the undressed hair did nothing to detract from her bearing. Her breeding.

'I serve,' she countered. 'And have all my life. I am Deirdre, queen of the Sea of Ice.'

When she closed the door behind her, he continued to stare. He'd heard of Rose Castle, the legend of it, in boyhood. The palace that stood on an island in what had once been a calm and pretty lake, edged by lush forests and rich fields. Betrayal, jealousy, vengeance, and witchcraft had doomed it all to an eternity of winter.

There was something about a rose trapped in a pillar of ice. He couldn't quite remember how it all went.

Such things were nonsense, of course. Entertaining stories to be told to a child at bedtime.

And yet . . . yet he'd traveled through that world of white

and bitter cold. He'd fought and won a battle, in high summer, then somehow had become lost in winter.

Because he, in his delirium, had traveled far north. Perhaps into the Lost Mountains or even beyond them, where the wild tribes hunted giant white bear and dragons still guarded caves.

He'd talked with men who claimed to have been there, who spoke of dark blue water crowded with islands of ice, and of warriors tall as trees.

But none had ever spoken of a castle.

How much had he imagined, or dreamed? Determined to see for himself, he tossed back the bedcovers. Sweat slicked his skin, and his muscles trembled, appalling him — scoring his pride — as the simple task of shifting to sit on the side of the bed sapped his strength. He sat for several moments more, gathering it back.

When he managed to stand, his vision wavered, as if he was looking through water. He felt his knees buckle but managed to grip the bedpost and stay on his feet.

While he waited to steady, he studied the room. It was simply appointed, he noted. Tasteful, certainly, even elegant in its way unless you looked closely enough to see that the fabrics were fraying with age. Still, the chests and the chairs gleamed with polish. While the rug was faded with time, its workmanship was lovely. The candlesticks were gleaming silver, and the fire burned quietly in a hearth carved from lapis.

As creakily, as carefully, as an aged grandfather, he walked across the room to the window.

Through it, as far as he could see, the world was white. The sun was a dim haze behind the white curtain that draped the sky, but it managed to sparkle a bit on the ice that surrounded the castle. In the distance, he saw the shadows of the forest, hints of black and gray smothered in snow. In the north, far north, mountains speared up. White against white.

Closer in, at the feet of the castle, the snow spread in sheets and blankets. He saw no movement, no tracks. No life.

Were they alone here? he wondered. He and the woman who called herself a queen?

Then he saw her, a regal flash of red against the white. She walked with a long, quick stride – as a woman might, he thought, bustle off to the market. As if she sensed him there, she stopped, turned. Looked up at his window.

He couldn't see her expression clearly, but the way her chin angled told him she was displeased with him. Then she turned away again, her fiery cloak swirling, as she continued over that sea toward the forest.

He wanted to go after her, to demand answers, explanations. But he could barely make it back to the bed before he collapsed. Trembling from the effort, he buried himself under the blankets again and slept the day away.

'My lady, he's demanding to see you again.'

Deirdre continued to work in the precious dirt under the wide dome. Her back ached, but she didn't mind it. In this, what she called her garden, she grew herbs and vegetables and a few precious flowers in the false spring generated by the sun through the glass.

'I have no time for him, Orna.' She hoed a trench. It was a constant cycle, replenishing, tending, harvesting. The garden was life to her world. And one of her few true pleasures. 'Between you and Cordelia he's tended well enough.'

Orna pursed her lips. She had nursed Deirdre as a babe, had tutored her, tended her, and since the death of Queen Fiona, had stood when she could as mother. She was one of the few in Rose Castle who dared to question the young queen.

'It's been three days since he woke. The man is restless.'

Deirdre straightened, rested her weight on the hoe. 'Is he in pain?'

Orna's weathered face creased with what might have

been impatience. 'He says not, but he's a man, after all. He has pain. Despite it, and his weakness, he won't be kept to his chamber much longer. The man is a prince, my lady, and used to being obeyed.'

'I rule here.' Deirdre scanned her garden. The earlier plantings were satisfactory. She couldn't have the lush, but she could have the necessary. Even, she thought as she looked at her spindly, sun-starved daisies, the occasional indulgence.

'One of the kitchen boys should gather cabbages for dinner,' she began. 'Have the cook choose two of the hens. Our guest needs meat.'

'Why do you refuse to see him?'

'I don't refuse.' Annoyed, Deirdre went back to her work. She was avoiding the next meeting, and she knew it. Something had come into her during the healing, something she was unable to identify. It left her uneasy and unsettled.

'I stayed with him three days, three nights,' she reminded Orna. 'It's put me behind in my duties.'

'He's very handsome.'

'So is his horse,' Deirdre said lightly. 'And the horse is of more interest to me.'

'And strong,' Orna continued, stepping closer. 'A prince from outside our world. He could be the one.'

'There is no one.' Deirdre tossed her head. Hope put no fuel in the fire nor food in the pot. It was a luxury she, above all, could ill afford. 'I want no man, Orna. I will depend on no one but myself. It's woman's foolishness, woman's need, and man's deceit that have cursed us.'

'Woman's pride as much as foolishness.' Orna laid a hand on the staff of the hoe. 'Will you let yours stop you from taking a chance for freedom?'

'I will provide for my people. When the time comes I will lie with a man until I conceive. I will make the next ruler, train the child as I was trained.'

'Love the child,' Orna murmured.

'My heart is so cold.' Tired, Deirdre closed her eyes. 'I fear there is no love in me. How can I give what isn't mine?'

'You're wrong.' Gently Orna touched her cheek. 'Your heart isn't cold. It's only trapped, as the rose is trapped in ice.'

'Should I free it, Orna, so it could be broken as my mother's was?' She shook her head. 'That solves nothing. Food must be put on the table, fuel must be gathered. Go now, tell our guest that I'll visit him in his chambers when time permits.'

'This seems like a fine time.' So saying, Kylar strode into the dome.

3

He'd never seen anything like the garden before. But then, Kylar had seen a great deal of the unexpected in Rose Castle in a short time. Such as a queen dressed in men's clothing – trousers and a ragged tunic. The result was odd, and strangely alluring. Her hair was tied back, but not with anything so female as a ribbon. She'd knotted it with a thin leather strap, such as he did himself when doing some quick spot of manual labor.

Her face was flushed from her work and as lovely as the

flower he'd first taken her for. She did not look pleased to see him. Even as he watched, her eyes chilled.

Behold the ice queen, he thought. A man would risk freezing off important parts of his body should he try to thaw her.

'I see you're feeling better, my lord.'

'If you'd spared me five minutes of your time, you'd have seen so before.'

'Will you pardon us, Orna.' She knelt and began to plant the long eyes of potatoes harvested earlier in the year. It was a distraction, one she needed. Seeing him again stirred her, in dangerous ways. 'You'll excuse me, my lord, if I continue with my task.'

'Are there no servants to do such things?'

'There are fifty-two of us in Rose Castle. We all have our places and our duties.'

He squatted beside her, though it caused his side to weep. Taking her hand, he turned it over and examined the ridge of callus. 'Then I would say, my lady, you have too many duties.'

'It's not for you to question me.'

'You don't give answers, so I must continue to question. You healed me. Why do you resent me?'

'I don't know. But I do know that I require both hands

for this task.' When he released her, she continued to plant. 'I'm unused to strangers,' she began. Surely that was it. She had never seen, much less healed, a stranger before. Wouldn't that explain why, after looking into his mind, into his heart, she felt so drawn to him?

And afraid of him.

'Perhaps my manners are unpolished, so I will beg your pardon for any slight.'

'They're polished diamond-bright,' he corrected. 'And stab at a man.'

She smiled a little. 'Some men, I imagine, are used to softer females. I thought Cordelia would suit your needs.'

'She's biddable enough, and pretty enough, which is why you have the dragon guarding her.'

Her smile warmed fractionally. 'Of course.'

'I wonder why I prefer you to either of them.'

'I couldn't say.' She moved down the row, and when he started to move with her, he gasped. She cursed. 'Stubborn.' She rose, reached down, and to his surprise, wrapped her arms around him. 'Hold on to me. I'll help you inside.'

He simply buried his face in her hair. 'Your scent,' he told her. 'It haunts me.'

'Stop it.'

'I can't get your face out of my head, even when I sleep.'

Her stomach fluttered, alarming her. 'Sir, I will not be trifled with.'

'I'm too damn weak to trifle with you.' Hating the unsteadiness, he leaned heavily against her. 'But you're beautiful, and I'm not dead.' When he caught his breath, he eased away. 'I should be. I've had time to think that through.' He stared hard into her eyes. 'I've seen enough battle to know when a wound is mortal. Mine was. How did I cheat death, Deirdre? Are you a witch?'

'Some would say.' Because his color concerned her, she unbent enough to put an arm around his waist. 'You need to sit before you fall. Come back inside.'

'Not to bed. I'll go mad.'

She'd tended enough of the sick and injured to know the truth of that. 'To a chair. We'll have tea.'

'God spare me. Brandy?'

She supposed he was entitled. She led him through a doorway, down a dim corridor away from the kitchen. She skirted the main hallway and moved down yet another corridor. The room where she took him was small, chilly, and lined floor to ceiling with books.

She eased him into a chair in front of the cold fireplace, then went over to open the shutters and let in the light.

'The days are still long,' she said conversationally as she

walked to the fireplace. This one was framed in smooth green marble. 'Planting needs to be finished while the sun can warm the seeds.'

She crouched in front of the fire, set the logs to light. 'Is there grass in your world? Fields of it?'

'Yes.'

She closed her eyes a moment. 'And trees that go green in spring?'

He felt a wrench in his gut. For home – and for her. 'Yes.'

'It must be like a miracle.' Then she stood, and her voice was brisk again. 'I must wash, and see to your brandy. You'll be warm by the fire. I won't be long.'

'My lady, have you never seen a field of grass?'

'In books. In dreams.' She opened her mouth again, nearly asked him to tell her what it smelled like. But she wasn't sure she could bear to know. 'I won't keep you waiting long, my lord.'

She was true to her word. In ten minutes she was back, her hair loose again over the shoulders of a dark green dress. She carried the brandy herself.

'Our wine cellars were well stocked once. My grandfather, I'm told, was shrewd in that area. And in this one,' she added, gesturing toward the books. 'He enjoyed a glass of good wine and a good book.'

'And you?'

'The books often, the wine rarely.'

When she glanced toward the door, he saw her smile, fully, warmly, for the first time. He could only stare at her as his throat went dry and his heart shuddered.

'Thank you, Magda. I would have come for it.'

'You've enough to do, my lady, without carting trays.' The woman seemed ancient to Kylar. Her face as withered as a winter apple, her body bowed as if she carried bricks on her back. But she set the tea tray on the sideboard and curtseyed with some grace. 'Should I pour for you, my lady?'

'I'll see to it. How are your hands?'

'They don't trouble me overmuch.'

Deirdre took them in her own. They were knotted and swollen at the joints. 'You're using the ointment I gave you?'

'Yes, my lady, twice daily. It helps considerable.'

Keeping her eyes on Magda's, Deirdre rubbed her thumbs rhythmically over the gnarled knuckles. 'I have a tea that will help. I'll show you how to make it, and you'll drink a cup three times a day.'

'Thank you, my lady.' Magda curtseyed again before she left the room.

Kylar saw Deirdre rub her own hands as if to ease a pain before she reached for the teapot. 'I'll answer your questions,

Prince Kylar, and hope that you'll answer some of mine in turn.' She brought him a small tray of cheese and biscuits, then settled into a chair with her tea.

'How do you survive?'

To the point, she thought. 'We have the garden. Some chickens and goats for eggs and milk, and meat when meat is needed. There's the forest for fuel and, if we're lucky, for game. The young are trained in necessary skills. We live simply,' she said, sipping her tea. 'And well enough.'

'Why do you stay?'

'Because this is my home. You risked your life in battle to protect yours.'

'How do you know I didn't risk it to take what belonged to someone else?'

She watched him over the rim of her cup. Yes, he was handsome. His looks were only more striking now that he'd regained some of his strength. One of the servants had shaved him, and without the stubble of beard he looked younger. But little less dangerous. 'Did you?'

'You know I didn't.' His gaze narrowed on her face. 'You know. How is that, Deirdre of the Ice?' He reached out, clamped a hand on her arm. 'What did you do to me during the fever?'

'Healed you.'

'With witchcraft?'

'I have a gift for healing,' she said evenly. 'Should I have used it, or let you die? There was no dark in it, and you are not bound to me for payment.'

'Then why do I feel bound to you?'

Her pulse jumped. His hand wasn't gripping her arm now. It caressed. 'I did nothing to tie you. I have neither desire nor the skill for it.' Cautiously, she moved out of reach. 'You have my word. When you're well enough to travel, you're free to go.'

'How?' It was bitter. 'Where?'

Pity stirred in her, swam into her eyes. She remembered the face of the woman in his mind, the love she'd felt flow between them. His mother, she thought. Even now watching for his return home.

'It won't be simple, nor without risk. But you have a horse, and we'll give you provisions. One of my men will travel with you as far as possible. I can do no more than that.'

He put it aside for now. When the time came, he would find his way home. 'Tell me how this came to be. This place. I've heard stories – betrayal and witchcraft and cold spells over a land that was once fruitful and at peace.'

'So I am told.' She rose again to stir the fire. 'When my grandfather was king, there were farms and fields. The land

165

was green and rich, the lake blue and thick with fish. Have you ever seen blue water?'

'I have, yes.'

'How can it be blue?' she asked as she turned. There was puzzlement on her face, and more, he thought. An eagerness he hadn't seen before. It made her look very young.

'I haven't thought about it,' he admitted. 'It seems to be blue, or green, or gray. It changes, as the sky changes.'

'My sky never changes.' The eagerness vanished as she walked to the window. 'Well,' she said, and straightened her shoulders. 'Well. My grandfather had two daughters, twin-born. His wife died giving them life, and it's said he grieved for her the rest of his days. The babes were named Ernia, who was my aunt, and Fiona, who was my mother, and on them he doted. Most parents dote on their children, don't they, my lord?'

'Most,' he agreed.

'So he did. Like their mother, they were beautiful, and like their mother, they were gifted. Ernia could call the sun, the rain, the wind. Fiona could speak to the beasts and the birds. They were, I'm told, competitive, each vying for their father's favor though he loved them both. Do you have siblings, my lord?'

'A brother and a sister, both younger.'

She glanced back. He had his mother's eyes, she thought. But her hair had been light. Perhaps his father had that ink-black hair that looked so silky.

'Do you love them, your brother and your sister?'

'Very much.'

'That is as it should be. But Ernia and Fiona could not love each other. Perhaps it was because they shared the same face, and each wanted her own. Who can say? They grew from girl to woman, and my grandfather grew old and ill. He wanted them married and settled before his death. Ernia he betrothed to a king in a land beyond the Elf Hills, and my mother he promised to a king whose lands marched with ours to the east. Rose Castle was to be my mother's, and the Palace of Sighs, on the border of the Elf Hills, my aunt's. In this way he divided his wealth and lands equally between them, for he was, I'm told, a wise and fair ruler and a loving father.'

She came back to sit and sip at tea gone cold. 'In the weeks before the weddings, a traveler came and was welcome here as all were in those days. He was handsome and clever, quick of tongue and smooth with charm. A minstrel by trade, it's said he sang like an angel. But fair looks are no mirror of the heart, are they?'

'A pleasant face is only a face.' Kylar lifted a shoulder. 'Deeds make a man.'

'Or woman,' she added. 'So I have always believed, and so, in this case, it was. In secret, this handsome man courted and seduced both twins, and both fell blindly in love with him. He came to my mother's bed, and to her sister's, bearing a single red rose and promises never meant to be kept. Why do men lie when women love?' The question took him aback. 'My lady . . . not all men are deceivers.'

'Perhaps not.' Though she was far from convinced. 'But he was. One evening the sisters, of the same mind, wandered to the rose garden. Each wanted to pluck a red rose for her lover. It was there the lies were discovered. Instead of comforting each other, instead of raging against the man who had deceived them both, they fought over him. She-wolves over an unworthy badger. Ernia's temper called the wind and the hail, and Fiona's had the beasts stalking out of the forest to snarl and howl.'

'Jealousy is both a flawed and a lethal weapon.'

She angled her head. Nodded. 'Well said. My grandfather heard the clamor and roused himself from his sick-bed. Neither marriage could take place now, as both his daughters were disgraced. The minstrel, who had not slipped away quickly enough, was locked in the dungeon until his punishment could be decided. There was weeping and wailing from the sisters, as that punishment would surely be banishment, if not death. But he was spared when it came to be known that my mother was with child. His child, for she had lain with no other.'

'You were the child.'

'Yes. So, by becoming, I saved my father's life. The grief of this, the shame of this, ended my grandfather's. Before he died, he ordered Ernia to the Palace of Sighs. Because of the child, he decreed that my mother would marry the minstrel. It was this that drove Ernia mad, and on the day the marriage took place, the day her own father died in despair, she cast her spell.

'Winter, endless years of it. A sea of ice to lock Rose Castle away from the world. The rosebush where flowers had been plucked from lies would not bear bud. The child her sister carried would never feel the warmth of summer sun on her face, or walk in a meadow or see a tree bear fruit. One faithless man, three selfish hearts, destroyed a world. And so became the Isle of Winter in the Sea of Ice.'

'My lady.' He laid a hand on hers. Her life, he thought, the whole of it had been spent without the simple comfort of sunlight. 'A spell cast can be broken. You have power.'

'My gift is of healing. I cannot heal the land.' Because she wanted to turn her hand over in his, link fingers, feel that connection, she drew away. 'My father left my mother before I was born. Escaped. Later, as she watched her people starve, my mother sent messengers to the Palace of Sighs to ask for a truce. To beg for one. But they never came back. Perhaps they died, or lost their way. Or simply rode on into the warmth and the sun. No one who has left here has ever come back. Why would they?'

'Ernia the Witch-Queen is dead.'

'Dead?' Deirdre stared into the fire. 'You're sure of this?'

'She was feared, and loathed. There was great celebration when she died. It was on the Winter Solstice, and I remember it well. She's been dead for nearly ten years.'

Deirdre closed her eyes. 'As her sister has. So they died together. How odd, and how apt.' She rose again to walk to the window. 'Ten years dead, and her spell holds like a clenched fist. How bitter her heart must have been.'

And the faint and secret hope she'd kept flickering inside that upon her aunt's death the spell would break, winked out. She drew herself up. 'What we can't change, we learn to be content with.' She stared out at the endless world of white. 'There is beauty here.'

'Yes.' It was Deirdre that Kylar watched. 'Yes. There is beauty here.'

4

He wanted to help her. More, Kylar thought, he wanted to save her. If there had been something tangible to fight – a man, a beast, an army – he would have drawn his sword and plunged into battle for her.

She moved him, attracted him, fascinated him. Her steady composure in the face of her fate stirred in him both admiration and frustration. This was not a woman to weep on a man's shoulder. It annoyed him to find himself wishing that she would, as long as the shoulder was his.

She was an extraordinary creature. He wanted to fight for her. But how did a man wage war on magic?

He'd never had any real experience with it. He was a soldier, and though he believed in luck, even in fate, he believed more in wile and skill and muscle.

He was a prince, would one day be a king. He believed in justice, in ruling with a firm touch on one hand and a merciful one on the other.

There was no justice here, where a woman who had done no wrong should be imprisoned for the crimes and follies and wickedness of those who had come before.

She was too beautiful to be shut away from the rest of the world. Too small, he mused, too fragile to work her hands raw. She should be draped in silks and ermine rather than homespun.

Already after less than a week on the Isle of Winter, he felt a restlessness, a need for color and heat. How had she stayed sane never knowing a single summer?

He wanted to bring her the sun.

She should laugh. It troubled him that he had not once heard her laugh. A smile, surprisingly warm when it was real enough to reach her eyes. That he had seen. He would find a way to see it again.

He waded through the snow across what he supposed

had once been a courtyard. Though his wound had troubled him on waking, he was feeling stronger now. He needed to be doing, to find some work or activity to keep his blood moving and his mind sharp. Surely there was some task, some bit of work he could undertake for her here. It would repay her in some small way, and serve to keep his mind and hands busy while his body healed.

He recalled the stag he'd seen in the forest. He would hunt, then, and bring her meat. The wind that had thrashed ceaselessly for days had finally quieted. Though the utter stillness that followed it played havoc with the nerves, it would make tracking through the forest possible.

He moved through a wide archway on the other side of the courtyard. And stopped to stare.

This, he realized with wonder, had been the rose garden. Gnarled and blackened stalks tangled out of the snow. Once, he imagined, it would have been magnificent, full of color and scent and humming bees.

Now it was a great field of snow cased in ice.

Bisecting that field were graceful paths of silver stone, and someone kept them clear. There were hundreds of bushes, all brittle with death, the stalks spearing out of their cold graves like blackened bones.

Benches, these, too, cleared of snow and ice, stood in

173

graceful curves of deep jewel colors. Ruby, sapphire, emerald, they gleamed in the midst of the stark and merciless white. There was a small pond in the shape of an open rose, and its flower held a rippled sheet of ice. Dead branches with vicious thorns strangled iron arbors. More spindly corpses climbed up the silver stone of the walls as if they'd sought to escape before winter murdered them.

In the center, where all paths led, was a towering column of ice. Under the glassy sheen, he could see the arch of blackened branches studded with thorns, and hundreds of withered flowers trapped forever in their moment of death.

The rosebush, he thought, where the flowers of lies had been plucked. No, he corrected as he moved toward it. More a tree, for it was taller than he was and spread wider than the span of both his arms. He ran his fingertips over the ice, found it smooth. Experimentally, he took the dagger from his belt, dragged its tip over the ice. It left no mark.

'It cannot be reached with force.'

Kylar turned and saw Orna standing in the archway. 'What of the rest? Why haven't the dead branches been cleared and used for fire?' he asked her.

'To do so would be to give up hope.' She had hope still, and more when she looked into Kylar's eyes.

She saw what she needed there. Truth, strength, and courage.

'She walks here.'

'Why would she punish herself in such a way?' he demanded.

'It reminds her, I think, of what was. And what is.' But not, Orna feared, of what might be. 'Once, when my lady was but eight, and the last of the dogs died, breaking her heart, she took her grandfather's sword. In her grief and temper, she tried to hack through that ice into the bush. For nearly an hour she stabbed and sliced and beat at it, and could not so much as scratch the surface. In the end, she went to her knees there where you stand now and wept as if she'd die from it. Something in her did die that day, along with the last of the dogs. I have not heard her weep since. I wish she would.'

'Why do you wish for your lady's tears?'

'For then she would know her heart is not dead but, like the rose, only waiting.'

He sheathed his dagger. 'If force can't reach it, what can?'

She smiled, for she knew he spoke of the heart as much as the rose. 'You will make a good king in your time, Kylar of Mrydon, for you listen to what isn't said. What can't be vanquished with sword or might can be won with truth, with love, with selflessness. She is in the stables, what is left of them. She wouldn't ask for your company, but would enjoy it.'

The stables lined three sides of another courtyard, but this one was crisscrossed with crooked paths dug through or trampled into the snow. Kylar saw the reason for it in the small troop of children waging a lively snow battle at the far end. Even in such a world, he thought, children found a way to be children.

As he drew closer to the stables, he heard the low cackle of hens. There were men on the roof, working on a chimney. They tipped their caps to him as he passed under the eaves and into the stables.

It was warmer, thanks to carefully banked fires, and clean as a parlor. The queen, he thought, tended her goats and chickens well. Iron kettles heated over the fires. Water for the stock, he concluded, made from melted snow. He noted barrows of manure. For use in her garden, he decided. A wise and practical woman, Queen Deirdre.

Then he saw the wise and practical woman, with her red hood tossed back, her gold hair raining down as she cooed up at his warhorse.

When the horse shook its great head and blew, she

laughed. The rich female sound warmed his blood more thoroughly than the fires.

'His name is Cathmor.'

Startled, embarrassed, Deirdre dropped the hands she'd lifted to stroke the horse's muzzle. She knew she shouldn't have lingered, that he would come check on his horse as it had been reported he did twice daily. But she'd so wanted to see the creature herself.

'You have a light step.'

'You were distracted.' He walked up beside her, and to her surprise and delight, the horse bumped his shoulder in greeting.

'Does that mean he's glad to see you?'

'It means he's hoping I have an apple.'

Deirdre fingered the small carrot from her garden she'd tucked in her pocket. 'Perhaps this will do.' She pulled it out, started to offer it to Kylar.

'He would enjoy being fed by a lady. No, not like that.' He took her hand and, opening it, laid the carrot on her palm. 'Have you never fed a horse?'

'I've never seen one.' She caught her breath as Cathmor dipped his head and nibbled the carrot out of her palm. 'He's bigger than I imagined, and more handsome. And softer.' Unable to resist, she stroked her hand down the horse's nose. 'Some of the children have been keeping him company. They'd make a pet of him if they could.'

'Would you like to ride him?'

'Ride?'

'He needs the exercise, and so do I. I thought I would hunt this morning. Come with me.'

To ride a horse? Just the idea of it was thrilling. 'I have duties.'

'I might get lost alone.' He brought her hand back up, ran it under his along Cathmor's silky neck. 'I don't know your forest. And I'm still a bit weak.'

Her lips twitched. 'Your wits are strong enough. I could send a man with you.'

'I prefer your company.'

To ride a horse, she thought again. How could she resist? Why should she? She was no fluttery girl who would fall into stutters and blushes by being alone with a man. Even this man.

'All right. What do I do first?'

'You wait until I saddle him.'

She shook her head. 'No, show me how to do it.'

When it was done, she sent one of the boys scurrying off to tell Orna she was riding out with the prince. She needn't have bothered, for as they walked the horse out of the stables, her people began to gather at the windows, in the courtyard.

When he vaulted into the saddle, they cheered him like a hero.

'It's been a long time since they've seen anyone ride,' she explained as Cathmor pranced in place. 'Some of them, like me, never have.' She let out a breath. 'It's a long way up.'

'Give me your hand.' He reached down to her. 'Trust me.'

She would have to if she wanted this amazing treat. She offered her hand, then yelped in shock when he simply hauled her up in the saddle in front of him.

'You might have warned me you intended to drag me up like a sack of turnips. If you've opened your wound again—'

'Quiet,' he whispered, entirely too close to her ear for comfort, and with her people cheering, he kicked Cathmor into a trot.

'Oh.' Her eyes popped wide as her bottom bounced. 'It's not what I expected.' And hardly dignified.

With shouts and whoops, children raced after them as they trotted out of the castle.

'Match the rhythm of your body to the gait of the horse,' he told her.

'Yes, I'm trying. Must you be so close?'

He grinned. 'Yes. And I'm enjoying it. You shouldn't be uneasy with a man, Deirdre, when you've seen him naked.'

'Seeing you naked hardly gives me cause to relax around you,' she shot back.

With a rolling laugh, he urged the horse to a gallop.

Her breath caught, but with delight rather than fear. Wind rushed by her cheeks, and snow flew up into the air like tattered lace. She closed her eyes for an instant to absorb the sensation, and the wild thrill made her dizzy.

So fast, she thought. So strong. When they charged up a hill she wanted to throw her arms in the air and shout for the sheer joy of it.

Her heart raced along with the horse, continued to pound even when they slowed at the verge of the forest that had been known as the Forgotten for the whole of her lifetime.

'It's like flying,' she mused. 'Oh, thank you.' She leaned down to press her cheek to the horse's neck. 'I'll never forget it. He's a grand horse, isn't he?'

Flushed with pleasure, she turned. His face was too close, so close she felt the warmth of his breath on her cheek. Close enough that she saw a kind of heat kindling in his eyes.

'No.' He caught her chin with his hand before she could turn away again. 'Don't. I kissed you before, when I thought I was dying.' His lips hovered a breath from hers. 'I lived.'

He had to taste her again; it seemed his sanity depended on it. But because he saw her fear, he took her mouth gently, skimming his lips over ones that trembled. Soothing as well as seducing. He watched her eyes go soft before her lashes fluttered down.

'Kiss me back, Deirdre.' His hand slid down until his arm could band her waist and draw her closer. 'This time kiss me back.'

'I don't know how.' But she already was.

Her limbs went weak, wonderfully weak, even as her pulse danced madly. Warmth enveloped her, reaching places inside that had never known its comfort.

The light that had sparked inside her when their hearts had brushed in healing spread.

On the Isle of Winter in the snowy rose garden, beneath a shield of ice, a tiny bud – tender green – formed on a blackened branch.

He nibbled at her lips until she parted them. And when he deepened the kiss she felt, for the first time in her life, a true lance of heat in her belly.

Yearning for more, she eased back, then indulged herself

by letting her head rest briefly on his shoulder. 'So it's this,' she whispered. 'It's this that makes the women sing in the kitchen in the morning.'

He stroked her hair, rubbed his cheek against it. 'It's a bit more than that.' Sweet, he thought. Strong. She was everything a man could want. Everything, he realized, that he wanted.

'Yes, of course.' She sighed once. 'More than that, but it starts like this. It can't for me.'

'It has.' He held her close when she would have drawn away. 'It did, the minute I saw you.'

'If I could love, it would be you. Though I'm not sure why, it would be you. If I were free, I would choose you.' She turned away again. 'We came to hunt. My people need meat.'

He fought the urge to yank her around, to plunder that lovely mouth until she yielded. Force wasn't the answer. So he'd been told. There were better ways to win a woman.

5

She spotted the tracks first. They moved soundlessly through the trees, and she was grateful for the need for silence.

How could she explain or ask him to understand, when she couldn't understand herself? Her heart was frozen, chilled to death by pride and duty, and the fear that she might do her people more harm.

Her father had made her in lies, then had run away from his obligation. Her mother had done her duty, and she had been kind. But her heart had been broken into so many pieces there had been none left for her child.

And what sort of child was it who could grieve more truly for a dead dog than for her own dead mother?

She had nothing emotionally to give a man, and wanted nothing from one. In that way she would survive, and keep her people alive.

Life, she reminded herself, mattered most. And what she felt for him was surely no more than a churning in the blood.

But how could she have known what it was like to be held by him? To feel his heart beat so strong and fast against hers? None of the books she'd read had captured with their clever words the true thrill of lips meeting.

Now that she understood, it would be just another precious memory, like a ride on horseback, to tuck away for the endless lonely nights.

She would decide later, she thought, if the nights were longer, lonelier, with the memory than they were without it.

But today she couldn't allow herself to think like a woman softened by a man's touch. She must think like a queen with people to provide for.

She caught the scent of the stag even before the horse

did, and held up a hand. 'We should walk from here,' she said under her breath.

He didn't question her, but dismounted, then reached up to lift her down. Then his arms were around her again, her hands on his shoulders, and her face tilted up to his. Even as she shook her head, he brushed his lips over her brow.

'Deirdre the fair,' he said softly. 'Such a pretty armful.'

The male scent of him blurred the scent of the stag. 'This is not the time.'

Because the catch in her voice was enough to satisfy him, for now, he reached over for his bow and quiver. But when she held out her hands for them, he lifted his eyebrows.

'The bow is too heavy a draw for you.' When she continued to stare, hands outstretched, he shrugged and gave them to her.

So, he thought, he would indulge her. They'd make do with more cabbage tonight.

Then he was left blinking as she tossed aside her cloak and streaked through the trees in her men's clothes like a wraith – soundless and swift. Before he could tether his horse, she'd vanished and he could do no more than follow in her tracks.

He stopped when he caught sight of her. She stood in the gloomy light, nearly hip-deep in snow. With a gesture smooth and polished as a warrior, she notched the arrow, drew back the heavy bow. The sharp *ping* of the arrow flying free echoed. Then she lowered the bow, and her head.

'Everyone misses sometimes,' he said as he started toward her.

Her head came up, her face cold and set. 'I did not miss. I find no pleasure in the kill. My people need meat.'

She handed the bow and quiver back to him, then trudged through the snow to where the stag lay.

Kylar saw she'd taken it down, fast, mercifully fast, with a single shot.

'Deirdre,' he called out. 'Do you ask yourself how game, even so sparse, come to be here where there is no food for them?'

She continued walking. 'My mother did what she could, leaving a call that would draw them to the forest. She hoped to teach me to do the same, but it's not my gift.'

'You have more than one,' he said. 'I'll get the horse.'

Once the deer was strapped onto the horse, Kylar cupped his hands to help Deirdre mount. 'Put your right foot in my hands, swing your left leg over the saddle.'

'There isn't room for both of us now. You ride, I'll walk.'

'No, I'll walk.'

'It's too far when you've yet to fully recover. Mount your horse.' She started to move past him, but he blocked her path. Her shoulders straightened like an iron bar. 'I said, mount. I am a queen, and you merely a prince. You will do as I bid.'

'I'm a man, and you merely a woman.' He shocked her speechless by picking her up and tossing her into the saddle. 'You'll do what you're told.'

However much she labored side by side with her people, no one had ever disobeyed a command. And no man had ever laid hands on her. 'You . . . *dare.*'

'I'm not one of your people.' He gathered the reins and began to walk the horse through the forest. 'Whatever our ranks, I'm as royal as you. Though that doesn't mean a damn at the moment. It's difficult to think of you as a queen when you're garbed like a man and I've seen you handle a bow that my own squire can barely manage. It's difficult to think of you as a queen, Deirdre,' he added with a glance back at her furious face, 'when I've held you in my arms.'

'Then you'd best remember what that felt like, for you won't be allowed to do so again.'

He stopped, and turning, ran his hand deliberately up her leg. When she kicked out at him, he caught her boot and laughed. 'Ah, so there's a temper in there after all. Good. I prefer bedding a woman with fire in her.'

Quick as a snake the dagger was out of her belt and in her hand. And its killing point at his throat. 'Remove your hand.'

He never flinched, but realized to his own shock that this wasn't merely a woman he could want. It was a woman he could love. 'Would you do it, I wonder? I think you might while the temper's on you, but then you'd regret it.' He brought his hand up slowly, gripped her knife hand by the wrist. 'We'd both regret it. I tell you I want to bed you. I give you the truth. Do you want lies?'

'You can bed Cordelia, if she's willing.'

'I don't want Cordelia, willing or not.' He took the knife from her hand, then brushed a kiss over her palm. 'But I want you, Deirdre. And I want you willing.' He handed her back the dagger, hilt first. 'Can you handle a sword as well as you do a dagger?'

'I can.'

'You're a woman of marvels, Deirdre the fair.' He began to walk again. 'I understand developing skill with the bow, but what need have you for sword or dagger?'

'Ignoring training in defense is careless and lazy. The training itself is good for the body and the mind. If my people are expected to learn how to handle a blade, then so should I be.'

'Agreed.'

When he paused a second time, her eyes narrowed in warning. 'I'm going to shorten the stirrups so you can ride properly. What happened to your horses?'

'Those who left the first year took them.' She ordered herself to relax and pleased herself by stroking Cathmor's neck again. 'There were cattle, too, and sheep. Those that didn't die of the cold were used as food. There were cottages and farmhouses, but people came to the castle for shelter, for food. Or wandered off hoping to find spring. Now they're under the snow and ice. Why do you want to bed me?'

'Because you're beautiful.'

She frowned down at him. 'Are men so simple, really?'

He laughed, shook his head, and her fingers itched to tangle in his silky black mane rather than the horse's. 'Simple enough about certain matters. But I hadn't finished the answer. Your beauty would be enough to make me want you for a night. Try this now, heels down. That's fine.'

He gave her foot a friendly pat, then walked back to the horse's head. 'Your strength and your courage add layers to beauty. They appeal to me. Your mind's sharp and cleaves clean. That's a challenge. And a woman who can plant potatoes like a farmwife and draw a dagger like an assassin is a fascinating creature.'

'I thought when a man wanted to pleasure himself with a woman, he softened her with pretty words and poetry and long looks full of pain and longing.'

What a woman, Kylar mused. He'd never seen the like of her. 'Would you like that?'

She considered it, and was relaxed again. It was easier to discuss the whole business as a practical matter. 'I don't know.'

'You wouldn't trust them.'

She smiled before she could stop it. 'I wouldn't, no. Have you bedded many women?'

He cleared his throat and began to walk a bit faster. 'That, sweetheart, isn't a question I'm comfortable answering.'

'Why not?'

'Because it's . . . it's a delicate matter,' he decided.

'Would you be more comfortable telling me if you've killed many men?'

'I don't kill for sport, or for pleasure,' he said, and his voice turned as frigid as the air. 'Taking a man's life is no triumph, my lady. Battle is an ugly business.'

'I wondered. I meant no offense.'

'I would have let them go.' He spoke so softly that she had to lean forward to hear clearly.

'Who?'

'The three who set upon me after the battle had been won. When I was for home. I would have let them pass in peace. What purpose was there in more blood?'

She'd already seen this inside him, and knew it for truth. He had not killed in hate nor in some fever of dark excitement. He had killed to live. 'They wouldn't let you pass in peace.'

'They were tired, and one already wounded. If I'd had an escort as I should, they would have surrendered. In the end, it was their own fear and my carelessness that killed them. I'm sorry for it.'

More for the waste of their lives, she realized, than for his own wounds. Understanding this, she felt something sigh inside her. 'Kylar.'

It was the first time she'd spoken his name, as she might to a friend. And she leaned down to touch his cheek with her fingertips, as she might touch a lover's.

'You'll rule well.'

She invited him to sup with her that night. Another first. He dressed in the fresh doublet Cordelia brought him, one of soft linen that smelled lightly of lavender and rosemary. He wondered from what chest it had been unearthed for his use, but as it fit well enough, he had no cause to complain.

But when he followed the servant into the dining hall, he wished for his court clothes.

She wore green again, but no simple dress of homespun. The velvet gown poured down her body, dipping low at the creamy rise of her breasts and sweeping out from her waist in soft, deep folds. Her hair was long and loose, but over it sparkled a crown glinting with jewels. More draped in shimmering ropes around her throat.

She stood in the glow of candlelight, beautiful as a vision, and every inch a queen.

When she offered a hand, he crossed to her, bowed deeply before touching his lips to her knuckles. 'Your Majesty.'

'Your Highness. The room,' she said with a gesture she hoped hid the nerves and pleasure she felt upon seeing the open approval on his face, 'is overlarge for two. I hope you'll be comfortable.'

'I see nothing but you.'

She titled her head. Curious, this flirting, she decided. And entertaining. 'Are these the pretty words and poetry?'

'They're the truth.'

'They fall pleasantly on the ear. It's an indulgence to have a fire in here,' she began as she let him escort her to the table. 'But tonight there is wine, and venison, and a welcome guest.'

At the head of the long table were two settings. Silver and crystal and linen white as the snow outside the windows. Behind them, the mammoth fire roared.

Servants slipped in to serve wine and the soup course. If he'd been able to tear his gaze away from Deirdre, he might have seen the glint in their eyes, the exchanged winks and quick grins.

She missed them as well, as she concentrated on the experience of her first formal meal with someone from outside her world. 'The fare is simple,' she began.

'As good as a bounty. And the company feeds me.'

She studied him thoughtfully. 'I do think I like pretty words, but I have no skill in holding a conversation with them.'

He took her hand. 'Why don't we practice?'

Her laugh bubbled out, but she shook her head. 'Tell me of your home, your family. Your sister,' she remembered. 'Is she lovely?'

'She is. Her name is Gwenyth. She married two years ago.'

'Is there love?'

'Yes. He was friend and neighbor, and they had a sweetness for each other since childhood. When I last saw her she was great with her second babe.' The faintest cloud passed over his face. 'I'd hoped to make my way home for the birthing.'

'And your brother?'

'Riddock is young, headstrong. He can ride like the devil.'

'You're proud of him.'

'I am. He'd give you poetry.' Kylar lifted his goblet. 'He has a knack for it, and loves nothing more than luring pretty maids out to the garden in the moonlight.'

She asked questions casually so he would talk. She was unsure of her conversational skills in this arena, and it was such a pleasure to just sit and listen to him speak so easily of things that were, to her, a miracle.

Summer and gardens, swimming in a pond, riding through a village where people went to market. Carts of glossy red apples – what would they taste like? Baskets of flowers whose scent she could only dream of.

She had a picture of his home now, as she had pictures in books.

She had a picture of him, and it was more than anything she'd ever found in a book.

Willing to pay whatever it cost her later, she lost herself in him, in the way his voice rose and fell, in his laugh. She thought she could sit this way for days, to talk like this with no purpose in it, no niggling worries. Just to be with him by the warmth of the fire, with wine sweet on her tongue and his eyes so intimately on hers.

She didn't object when he took her hand, when his fingers toyed with hers. If this was flirtation, it was such a lovely way to pass the time.

They spoke of faraway lands and cultures. Of paintings and of plays.

'You've put your library to good use,' he commented. 'I've known few scholars as well read.'

'I can see the world through books, and lives through the stories. Once a year, on Midsummer, we put on a pageant. We have music and games. I choose a story, and everyone takes a part as if it were a play. Surviving isn't enough. There must be life and color.'

There were times, secretly, when she pined near weeping for true color.

'All the children are taught to read,' she continued, 'and to do sums. If you have only a window on the world, you must look out of it. One of my men – well, he's just a boy really – he makes stories. They're quite wonderful.'

She caught herself, surprised at the sound of her own voice rambling. 'I've kept you long enough.'

'No.' His hand tightened on hers. He was beginning to realize it would never be long enough. 'Tell me more. You play music, don't you? A harp. I heard you playing, singing. It was like a dream.'

'You were feverish. I play a little. Some skill inherited from my father, I suppose.'

'I'd like to hear you play again. Will you play for me, Deirdre?'

'If you like.'

But as she started to rise, one of the men who'd helped serve rushed in. 'My lady, my lady, it's young Phelan!'

'What's happened?'

'He was playing with some of the boys on the stairs, and fell. We can't wake him. My lady, we fear he's dying.

6

A fraid to move him, they'd left the boy covered with a blanket at the base of the stairs. At first glance, Kylar thought the child, for he was hardly more, was already dead. He'd seen enough of death to recognize its face.

He judged the boy to be about ten, with fair hair and cheeks still round with youth. But those cheeks were gray, and the hair was matted with blood.

Those who circled and knelt around the boy made way when Deirdre hurried through.

'Get back now,' she ordered. 'Give him room.'

Before Deirdre could kneel, a weeping woman broke free to fall at her feet and clutch at her skirts with bloodstained hands. 'My baby. Oh, please, my lady! Help my little boy.'

'I will, Ailish. Of course I will.' Knowing that time was precious, Deirdre bent down and firmly loosened the terrified woman's hold on her. 'You must be strong for him, and trust. Let me see to him now.'

'He slipped, my lady.' Another youth came forward with a jerky step. His eyes were dry, but huge, and there were tracks of tears still drying on his cheeks. 'We were playing horse and rider on the stairs, and he slipped.'

'All right.' Too much grief, she thought, feeling waves of it pressing over her. Too much fear. 'It's all right now. I'll tend to him.'

'Deirdre.' Kylar kept his voice low, so only she could hear over the mother's weeping. 'There's nothing you can do here. I can smell death on him.'

As could she, and so she knew she had little time. 'What is the smell of death but the smell of fear?' She ran her hands gently over the crumpled body, feeling the hurts, finding so much broken in the little boy that her heart ached from it. Medicines would do no good here, but still her face was composed as she looked up.

'Cordelia, fetch my healing bag. Make haste. The rest, please, leave us now. Leave me with him. Ailish, go now.'

'Oh, no, please, my lady. Please, I must stay with my boy.'

'Do you trust me?'

'My lady.' She gripped Deirdre's hand, wept on it. 'I do.'

'Then do as I bid you. Go now and pray.'

'His neck,' Kylar began, then broke off when Deirdre whipped her head around and stared at him.

'Be silent! Help me or go, but don't question me.'

When Ailish was all but carried away, and the two of them were alone with the bleeding boy, Deirdre closed her eyes. 'This will hurt him. I'm sorry for it. Hold him down, hold him as still as you can, and do nothing to interfere. Nothing, do you understand?'

'No.' But Kylar shifted until he could clamp the boy's arms.

'Block thoughts of death from your mind,' she ordered. 'And fear, and doubt. Block them out as you would in battle. There's too much dark here already. Can you do this?'

'I can.' And because she asked it of him, Kylar let the cold come into him, the cold that steeled the mind to face combat.

'Phelan,' she said. 'Young Phelan, the bard.' Her voice was soft, almost a crooning as she traced her hands over him again. 'Be strong for me.'

She knew him already, had watched him grow and learn and be. She knew the sound of his voice, the quick flash of his grin, the lively turn of his mind. He had been hers, as all in Rose Castle were hers, from the moment of his first breath.

And so she merged easily with him.

While her hands worked, stroking, kneading, she slid into his mind. She felt his laughter inside her as he pranced and raced with his friends up and down the narrow stone steps. Felt his heart leap inside her own as his feet slipped. Then the fear, oh, the terror, an instant only before the horrible pain.

The snap of bone made her cry out softly, had her head rearing back. Something inside her crushed like thin clay under a stone hammer, and the sensation was beyond torment.

Her eyes were open now, Kylar saw. A deep and too brilliant green. Her breath came fast and hard, sweat pearled on her brow. And the boy screamed thinly, straining under his grip.

Both made a sound of agony as she slid a hand under the boy to cup his neck, laid her other on his heart. Both shuddered. Both went pale as death.

Kylar started to call out to her, to reach for her as she swayed. But he felt the heat, a ferocious fist of it that seemed to pump out of her, into the boy until the arms he held were like sticks of fire.

And the boy's eyes opened, stared up blindly.

'Take, young Phelan.' Her voice was thick now, echoed richly off the stone. 'Take what you need. Fire of healing.' She leaned down, laid her lips gently on his. 'Live. Stay with us. Your mother needs you.'

As Kylar watched, thunderstruck, color seeped back into the boy's face. He would have sworn he felt death skitter back into the shadows.

'My lady,' the boy said, almost dreamily. 'I fell.'

'Yes, I know. Sleep now.' She brushed her hand over his eyes, and they closed on a sigh. 'And heal. Let his mother in, if you will,' she said to Kylar. 'And Cordelia.'

'Deirdre—'

'Please.' The weakness threatened to drag her under, and she wanted to be away, in her own chamber before she lost herself to it. 'Let them in so I can tell them what must be done for him.'

She stayed kneeling when Kylar rose. The sounds of her people were like the dull roar of the ocean in her head. Even as Ailish collapsed next to her son, to gather him close to kiss Deirdre's now trembling hand, Deirdre gave clear, careful instructions for his care.

'Enough!' Alarmed by her pallor, Kylar swept her off the floor and into his arms. 'Tend the boy.'

'I'm not finished,' Deirdre managed.

'Yes, by the blood, you are.' The single glance he swept over those gathered challenged any to contradict him. 'Where is your chamber?'

'This way, my lord prince.' Orna led him through a doorway, down a corridor to another set of stairs. 'I know what to do for her, my lord.'

'Then you'll do it.' He glanced down at Deirdre as he carried her up the stairs. She had swooned after all, he noted. Her skin was like glass, her eyes closed. The boy's blood was on her hands. 'What did she risk by snatching the boy from death?'

'I cannot say, my lord.' She opened a door, hurried across a chamber to the bed. 'I will care for her now.'

'I stay.'

Orna pressed her lips together as he laid Deirdre on the bed. 'I must undress her. Wash her.'

Struggling with temper, he turned to stalk to the window. 'Then do so. Is this what she did for me?'

'I cannot say.' Orna met his eyes directly when he turned back. 'She did not speak of it to me. She does not speak of it with anyone. Prince Kylar, I will ask you to turn your back until my lady is suitably attired in her night garb.'

'Woman, her modesty is not an issue with me.' But he turned, stared out the window.

He had heard of those who could heal with the mind. But he had not believed it, not truly believed, before tonight. Nor had he considered what price the healer paid to heal.

'She will sleep,' Orna said some time later.

'I won't disturb her.' He came to the bed now, gazed down. There was still no color in her cheeks, but it seemed to him her breathing was steadier. 'Nor will I leave her.'

'My lady is strong, as valiant as ten warriors.'

'If I had ten as valiant, there would never be another battle to fight.'

Pleased with his response, Orna inclined her head. 'And my lady has, despite what she believes, a tender heart.' Orna set a bottle and goblet on the table near the bed. 'See that you don't bruise it. When she wakes, give her some of this tonic. I will not be far, should you need me.'

Alone, Kylar drew a chair near the bed and watched Deirdre sleep. For an hour, and then two. She was motionless and pale as marble in the firelight, and he feared she would never wake but would sleep like the beauty in another legend, for a hundred years.

Even days before he would have deemed such things

foolishness, stories for children. But now, after what he'd seen, what he'd felt, anything seemed possible.

Still, side by side with the worry inside him, anger bloomed. She had risked her life. He had seen death slide its cold fingers over her. She had bargained her life for the child's.

And, he was sure now, for his own.

When she stirred, just the slightest flutter of her lashes, he poured the tonic Orna had left into the cup.

'Drink this.' He lifted her head from the pillow. 'Don't speak. Just drink now.'

She sipped, and sighed. The hand she lifted to his wrist slid limply away again. 'Phelan?' she whispered.

'I don't know.' He brought the cup to her lips a second time. 'Drink more.'

She obeyed, then turned her head. 'Ask. Ask how young Phelan fares. Please. I must be sure.'

'Drink first. Drink it all.'

She did as he bade, and kept her eyes open and on his now. If she'd had the strength, she would have gone to find out herself. But the weakness was still dragging at her, and she could only trust Kylar to the task. 'Please. I won't be easy until I know his condition.'

Kylar set the empty cup aside, then crossed the chamber

to the door. Orna sat on a chair in the corridor, sewing by candlelight. She glanced up when she saw him. 'Tell my lady not to fret. Young Phelan is resting. Healing.' She got to her feet. 'If you would like to retire, my lord, I will sit with my lady.'

'Go to your bed,' he said shortly. 'I stay with her tonight.'

Orna bowed her head and hid a smile. 'As you wish.'

He stepped back inside, closed the door. And turning saw that Deirdre was sitting up in bed, with her hair spilling like honey over the white lawn of her nightdress.

'Your boy is resting, and well.'

At his words, he saw color return to her face, watched the dullness clear from her eyes. He came to the foot of the bed, which was draped in deep red velvet. 'You recover quickly, madam.'

'The tonic is potent.' Indeed she now felt clear of mind, and even the echoes of pain were fading from her body. 'Thank you for your help. His mother and father would have been too distraught to assist. Their worry could have distracted me. More, fear feeds death.'

She glanced around the room, a little warily. Orna hadn't laid out her nightrobe. 'If you'd excuse me now, I'll go see for myself.'

'Not tonight.'

To her shock he sat on the side of the bed near her. Only pride kept her from shifting over, or tugging up the blankets.

'I have questions.'

'I've answered several of your questions already.'

He lifted his brows. 'Now I have more. The boy was dying. His skull crushed, his neck damaged if not broken. His left arm was shattered.'

'Yes,' she said calmly. 'And inside his body, more was harmed. He bled inside himself. So much blood for such a little boy. But he has a strong heart, our Phelan. He is particularly precious to me.'

'He would have been dead in minutes.'

'He is not dead.'

'Why?'

'I can't answer.' Restlessly, she pushed at her hair. 'I can't explain it to you.'

'Won't.'

'Can't.'

When she would have turned her face away, he caught her chin, held it firmly. 'Try.'

'You overstep,' she said stiffly. 'Continually.'

'Then you should be growing accustomed to it. I held the boy,' he reminded her. 'I watched, and I felt life come back into him. Tell me what you did.'

She wanted to dismiss him, but he had helped her when she'd needed his help. So she would try. 'It's a kind of search, and a merging. An opening of both.' She lifted a hand, let it fall. 'It is a kind of faith, if you will.'

'It caused you pain.'

'Do you think fighting death is painless? You know better. To heal, I must feel what he feels, and bring him up ...' She shook her head, frustrated with words. 'Take him back to the pain. Then we ride it together, so that I see, feel, know.'

'You rode more than pain. You rode death. I saw you.'

'We were stronger.'

'And if you hadn't been?'

'Then death would have won,' she said simply. 'And a mother would be grieving her firstborn tonight.'

'And you? Deirdre of the Ice, would your people be grieving you?'

'There is a risk. Do you turn from battle, Kylar? Or do you face it knowing your life might be the price paid at end of day? Would you not stand for any one of your people if they had need? Would you expect me to do less for one of mine?'

'I was not one of yours.' He took her hand before she could look away. 'You rode death with me, Deirdre. I remember. I thought it a dream, but I remember. The pain, as if the sword cut into me fresh. That same pain mirrored in your eyes as you looked down at me. The heat of your body, the heat of your life pouring into me. I was nothing to you.'

'You were a man. You were hurt.' She reached out now, laying her hand on his cheek. 'Why are you angry? Should I have let you die because my medicines weren't enough to save you? Should I have stepped back from you and my own gift because it would cause me a moment's pain to save you? Does your pride bleed now because a woman fought for your life?'

'Perhaps it does.' He closed his hand over her wrist. 'When I carried you in here I thought you would die, and I was helpless.'

'You stayed with me. That was kind.'

He made some sound, then pushed himself off the bed to pace. 'When a man goes into battle, Deirdre, it's sword to sword, lance to lance, fist to fist. These are tangible things. What you've done, magic or miracle, is so much more. And you were right. I can't understand it.'

'It changes how you think of me.'

'Yes.'

She lowered her lashes, hid the fresh pain. 'There is no

shame in it. Most men would not have stayed to help, certainly not have stayed to speak with me. I'm grateful. Now if you'd excuse me, I'd like to be alone.'

Slowly, he turned back to her. 'You misunderstand me. Before I thought of you as a woman – beautiful, strong, intelligent. Sad. Now I think of you as all of that, and so much more. You humble me. You expect me to step away from you, because of all you are. I can't. I want to be with you, and I have no right.'

With her heart unsteady, she looked at him again. 'Is it gratitude that draws you to me?'

'I am grateful. I owe you for every breath I take. But it isn't gratitude I feel when I look at you.'

She slid out of bed to stand on her own feet. 'Is it desire?'

'I desire you.'

'I've never had a man's arms around me in love. I want them to be yours.'

'What right do I have when I can't stay with you? I should already be gone. Both my family and my people wait.'

'You give me truth, and truth means more than pretty words and empty promises. I wondered about this, and now I know. When I healed you I felt something I've never felt before. Mixed with the pain and the cold that comes into me so bitter there was . . . light.'

Watching him, she spread her hands. 'I said I did nothing to bind you to me, and that is truth. But something happened in me when I was part of you. It angered me, and it frightened me. But now, just now . . . ' She drew a breath and spoke without a blush. 'It excites me. I've been so cold. Give me one night of warmth. You said you wanted me willing.' She reached up, tugged the ribbons loose from the bodice of the nightdress. 'And I am,' she said as the white gown slid down to pool at her feet.

7

S he was a vision. More than he could have dreamed. Slim and small, she stood in the glow of candle and firelight.

'Will you give me a night?' she asked him.

'Deirdre. My love. I would give you a lifetime.'

'I want no pledges that can't be kept, no words but truth. Only give me what can be, and it will be enough,' she replied somberly.

'My lady.' He felt, somehow, that the step toward her was the most momentous of his life. And when he took her hands, that he was taking the world. 'It is the truth. Why or how I don't know. But never have I spoken cleaner truth.'

She believed he meant it, in this time. In this place. 'Kylar, lifetimes are for those who are free.'

So she would be, he promised himself. Whatever had to be done. But now wasn't for plans and battles. 'If you won't accept that pledge, let me pledge this. That I have loved no other as I love you tonight.'

'I can give that vow back to you. I thought it would be for duty.' She lifted her hands to his face, traced the shape of it with her fingers. 'And I thought the first time, it would be with fear.' She laughed a little. 'My heart jumps. Can you feel it?'

He laid a hand on her breast, felt the shiver. Felt the leap. 'I won't hurt you.'

'Oh, no.' She laid a hand on his heart in turn. They had brushed once before, she thought. Heart to heart. Nothing had been the same for her since. Nothing would be the same for her ever again. 'You won't hurt me. Warm me, Kylar, as a man warms his woman.'

He drew her into his arms. Gently, gently. Laid his lips on hers. Tenderly. There once more, she thought. There. That miracle of mouth against mouth. Sighing out his name, she let herself melt into the kiss.

'The first time you kissed me, I thought you were foolish.'

His lips curved on hers. 'Did you?'

'Half frozen and bleeding, and you would waste your last breath flirting with a woman. Such is a man.'

'Not a waste,' he corrected. 'But I can do better now.' With a flourish that pleased them both, he swept her into his arms. 'Come to bed, my lady.'

As she had once longed to do, she toyed with his silky black hair. 'You must teach me what to do.'

His muscles tightened, nerves and thrills, at the thought of her innocence. Tonight she would give him what she had given no other. In the candle glow he saw her face, saw that she gave him this treasure without fear, without shame.

No, he would not hurt her, but would do all in his power to bring her joy.

He laid her on the bed, rubbed his cheek against hers. 'It will be my pleasure to instruct you.'

'I've seen the goats mate.'

His burst of laughter was muffled in her hair. 'This, I can promise, will be somewhat different than the mating of goats. So pay attention,' he said, grinning now as he lifted his head, 'while I give you your first lesson.'

He was a patient teacher, and surely, she thought as her

skin began to shiver and sing under his hands, a skilled one. His mouth drank from hers, deep, then deeper until it was how she imagined it might be to slide bonelessly into a warm river.

Surrounded, floating, then submerged.

His hands roamed over her breasts, then cupped them as if he could hold her heartbeat in his palms. The sensation of those strong, hard hands on her flesh shimmered straight down to her belly. His mouth skimmed the side of her throat, nibbling.

'How lovely.' She murmured it, arching a little to invite more. 'How clever for breasts to give pleasure as well as milk.'

'Indeed.' His thumbs brushed over her nipples, and made her gasp. 'I've often thought the same.'

'Oh ... but what do I ... ' Her words, her thoughts trailed off into a rainbow when that nibbling mouth found her breast.

She made a sound in her throat, half cry, half moan. It thrilled him, that sound of shocked pleasure, the sudden shudder of her body, the quick jolt of her heart under his lips. As she arched again, her fingers combed through his hair, gripped there and pressed him closer. The sweet taste of her filled him like warmed wine.

He rose over her to tug his doublet aside, but before he could satisfy himself with that glorious slide of his flesh to her flesh, she lifted her hands, ran them experimentally over his chest.

'Wait.' She needed to catch her breath. It was all running through her so quickly that it nearly blurred. She wanted everything, but clearly, so that she might remember each stroke, each taste, each moment.

'I touched you when you were hurt. But this is different. I looked at your body, but didn't see it as I do now.' Carefully she traced her finger along the scar running up his side. 'Does this trouble you?'

He felt the line of heat, took her hand quickly. 'No.' Even now, he thought, she would try to heal. 'There will be no pain tonight, for either of us.'

He lowered to her, took her mouth again. There was a hint of urgency now, a taste of need. So much to feel, she mused dreamily. So much to know. And with the warmth of him coursing through her, she enfolded him. There was a freedom here, she discovered, in being about to touch him, stroke, explore, with no purpose other than pleasure. The hard muscles, the pucker in his smooth skin that was a scar of battle.

The strength of him excited her, challenged her own so

that her hands, her mouth, her movements under him became more demanding.

This was fire, she realized. The first true licks of flame that brought nothing but delight and a bright, blinding need for more.

'I'm not fragile.' Indeed she felt alive with power, nearly frantic with a kind of raging hunger. 'Show me more. Show me all.'

No matter how his blood swam, he would be careful with her. But he could show her more. His hands roamed down her body, over her thighs. As if she knew what they both needed, she opened to him. Her breath came short, shivering out with quick little moans. Her nails bit into his back as she began to writhe under him.

He lifted his head and watched her fly over that first peak of pleasure.

Heat, such heat. She had never known such fire outside of healing magic. And this, somehow, this went deeper, spread wider. Her body was like a single wild flame. She cried out, the wanton sound of her own voice another shock to her system. Beyond control, beyond reason, she gripped his hips and called out his name.

When he plunged into her, the glory of it was like a shaft of lightning, bright and brilliant. There was a storm of those glorious and violent shocks as he thrust inside her. She locked herself around him, her face pressed against his neck and repeated his name as that miraculous heat consumed her.

'Sweetheart.' When he could speak again, he did so lazily, with his head nuzzled between her breasts. 'You are the most clever of students.'

She felt golden, beautiful, and for the first time in her memory, more woman than queen. For one night, she told herself, one miraculous night, she would be a woman.

'I'm sure I could do better, my lord, with a few more lessons.'

She was flushed, all but glowing, and her hair was a tangle of honeyed ropes over the white linen. 'I believe you're right.' He grinned and nibbled his way up her throat, lingered over her lips, then shifted so that she lay curled beside him.

'I'm so warm,' she told him. 'I never knew what it was like to be so warm. Tell me, Kylar, what's it like to have the sun on your face, full and bright?'

'It can burn.'

'Truly?'

'Truly.' He began to toy with her hair. 'And the skin

217

reddens or browns from it.' He ran a fingertip down her arm. Pale as milk, soft as satin. 'It can dazzle the eyes.' He turned so he could look down at her. 'You dazzle mine.'

'There was an old man who was my tutor when I was a child. He'd been all over the world. He told me of great tombs in a desert where the sun beat like fury, of green hills where flowers bloomed wild and the rain came warm. Of wide oceans where great fish swam that could swallow a boat whole and dragons with silver wings flew. He taught me so many marvelous things, but he never taught me the wonders that you have tonight.'

'There's never been another. Not like you. Not like this.'

Because she read the truth in his eyes, she drew him closer. 'Show me more.'

As they loved, inside a case of ice, the first green bud on a blackened stalk unfurled to a single tender leaf. And a second began to form.

When he woke, she was gone. At first he was baffled, for he slept like a soldier, and a soldier slept light as a cat. But he could see she had stirred the fire for him and had left his clothes folded neatly on the chest at the foot of the bed.

It occurred to him that he'd slept only an hour or two, but obviously like the dead. The woman was tireless – bless her – and had demanded a heroic number of lessons through the night.

A pity, he mused, she hadn't lingered in bed a bit longer that morning. He believed he might have managed another.

He rose to draw back the hangings on the windows. He judged it to be well into the morning, as her people were about their chores. He couldn't tell the time by the light here, for it varied so little from dawn to dusk. It was always soft and dull, with that veil of white over sky and sun. Even now a thin snow was falling.

How did she bear it? Day after day of cold and gloom. How did she stay sane, and more – content? Why should so good and loving a queen be cursed to live her life without warmth?

He turned, studied the chamber. He'd paid little attention to it the night before. He'd seen only her. Now he noted that she lived simply. The fabrics were rich indeed, but old and growing thin.

There had been silver and crystal in the dining hall, he recalled, but here her candlestands were of simple metal, the bowl for her washing a crude clay. The bed, the chest, the wardrobe were all beautifully worked with carved roses. But there was only a single chair and table.

He saw no pretty bottles, no silks, no trinket boxes.

She'd seen to it that the appointments in his guest chamber were suited to his rank, but for herself, she lived nearly as spartanly as a peasant.

His mother's ladies had more fuss and fancy in their chambers than this queen. Then he glanced at the fire and with a clutching in his belly realized she would have used much of the furniture for fuel, and fabric for clothes for her people.

She'd worn jewels when they dined. Even now he could see how they gleamed and sparkled over her. But what good were diamonds and pearls to her? They couldn't be sold or bartered, they put no food on the table.

A diamond's fire brought no warmth to chilled bones.

He washed in the bowl of water she'd left for him, and dressed.

There on the wall he saw the single tapestry, faded with age. Her rose garden, in full bloom, and as magnificent in silk thread as he'd imagined it. Alive with color and shape, it was a lush paradise caught in a lush moment of summer.

There was a figure of a woman seated on the jeweled bench beneath the spreading branches of the great bush that bloomed wild and free. And a man knelt at her feet, offering a single red rose.

He trailed his fingers over the threads and thought he would give his life and more to be able to offer her one red rose.

He was directed by a servant to Phelan's room, where the young bard had his quarters with a gaggle of other boys. The other boys gone, Phelan was sitting up in the bed with Deirdre for company. The chamber was small, Kylar noted, simple, but warmer by far than the queen's own.

She was urging a bowl of broth on Phelan and laughing in delight at the faces he made.

'A toad!'

'No, my lady. A monkey. Like the one in the book you lent me.' He bared his teeth and made her laugh again.

'Even a monkey must eat.'

'They eat the long yellow fruit.'

'Then you'll pretend this is the long yellow fruit.' She snuck a spoonful in his mouth.

He grimaced. 'I don't like the taste.'

'I know, the medicine spoils it a bit. But my favorite monkey needs to regain his strength. Eat it for me, won't you?'

'For you, my lady.' On a heavy sigh, the boy took the bowl and spoon himself. 'Then can I get up and play?'

'Tomorrow, you may get up for a short while.'

'My lady.' There was a wealth of horror and grief in the tone. Kylar could only sympathize. He'd once been a small boy and knew the tedium of being forced to stay idle in bed.

'A wounded soldier must recover to fight another day,' Kylar said as he crossed to the bed. 'Were you not a soldier when you rode the horse on the stairs?'

Phelan nodded, staring up at Kylar as it fascinated. To him the prince was as magnificent and foreign as every hero in every story he'd ever heard or read. 'I was, my lord.'

'Well, then. Do you know your lady kept me abed three full days when I came to her wounded?' He sat on the edge of the bed, leaned over and sniffed at the bowl. 'And forced the same broth on me. It's a cruelty, but a soldier bears such hardships.'

'Phelan will not be a soldier,' Deirdre said firmly. 'He is a bard.'

'Ah.' Kylar inclined his head in a bow. 'There is no man of more import than a bard.'

'More than a soldier?' Phelan asked, with eyes wide.

'A bard tells the tales and sings the songs. Without him, we would know nothing.'

'I'm making a story about you, my lord.' Excited now, Phelan spooned up his broth. 'About how you came from beyond, traveled the Forgotten wounded and near death, and how my lady healed you.'

'I'd like to hear the story when you've finished it.'

'You can make the story while you rest and recover.' Pleased that the bowl was empty, Deirdre took it as she stood, then leaned over to kiss Phelan's brow.

'Will you come back, my lady?'

'I will. But now you rest, and dream your story. Later, I'll bring you a new book.'

'Be well, young bard.' Kylar took Deirdre's hand to lead her out.

'You rose early,' he commented.

'There's much to be done.'

'I find myself jealous of a ten-year-old boy.'

'Nearly twelve is Phelan. He's small for his age.'

'Regardless, you didn't sit and feed me broth or kiss my brow when I was well enough to sit up on my own.'

'You were not so sweet-natured a patient.'

'I would be now.' He kissed her, surprised that she didn't flush and flutter as females were wont to do. Instead she answered his lips with a reckless passion that stirred his appetite. 'Put me to bed, and I'll show you.'

She laughed and nudged him back. 'That will have to wait. I have duties.'

'I'll help you.'

Her face softened. 'You have helped me already. But come. I'll give you work.'

8

There was no lack of work. The prince of Mrydon found himself tending goats and chickens. Shoveling manure, hauling endless buckets of snow to a low fire, carting precious wood to a communal pile.

The first day he labored he tired so quickly that it scored his pride. On the second, muscles that had gone unused during his recovery ached continually.

But the discomfort had the benefit of Deirdre rubbing him everywhere with one of her balms. And made the ensuing loving both merry and slippery.

She was a joy in bed, and he saw none of the sadness in her eyes there. Her laughter, the sound he'd longed to hear, came often.

He grew to know her people and was surprised and impressed by the lack of bitterness in them. He thought them more like a family, and though some were lazy, some grim, they shouldered together. They knew, he realized, that the survival of the whole depended on each.

That, he thought, was another of Deirdre's gifts. Her people held the will to go on, day after day, because their lady did. He couldn't imagine his own soldiers bearing the hardships and the tedium with half as much courage.

He came upon her in her garden. Though the planting and maintenance there was divided, as all chores were in Rose Castle, he knew she often chose to work or walk there alone.

She did so now, carefully watering her plantings with snowmelt.

'Your goat herd has increased by one.' He glanced down at his stained tunic. 'It's the first such birthing I've attended.'

Deirdre straightened, eased her back. 'The kid and the she-goat are well?'

'Well and fine, yes.'

'Why wasn't I called?'

'There was no need. Here, let me.' He took the spouted bucket from her. 'Your people work hard, Deirdre, but none as hard as their queen.'

'The garden is a pleasure to me.'

'So I've seen.' He glanced up at the wide dome. 'A clever device.'

'My grandfather's doing.' Since he was watering, she knelt and began to harvest turnips. 'He inherited a love for gardening from his mother, I'm told. It was she who designed and planted the rose garden. I'm named for her. When he was a young man, he traveled, and he studied with engineers and scientists and learned much. I think he was a great man.'

'I've heard of him, though I thought it all legend.' Kylar looked back at her as she placed turnips in a sack. 'It's said he was a sorcerer.'

Her lips curved a little. 'Perhaps. Magic may come through the blood. I don't know. I do know he gathered many of the books in the library, and built this dome for his mother when she was very old. Here she could start seedlings before the planting time and grow the flowers she loved, even in the cold. It must have given her great pleasure to work here when her roses and other flowers were dormant with winter.'

She sat back on her heels, looked over her rows and beyond to the sad and spindly daisies she prized like rubies. 'I wonder if somehow he knew that his gift to his mother would one day save his people from starvation.'

'You run low on fuel.'

'Yes. The men will cut another tree in a few days.' It always pained her to order it. For each tree cut meant one fewer left. Though the forest was thick and vast, without new growth there would someday be no more.

'Deirdre, how long can you go on this way?'

'As long as we must.'

'It's not enough.' Temper that he hadn't realized was building inside him burst out. He cast the bucket aside and grabbed her hands.

She'd been waiting for this. Through the joy, through the sweetness, she'd known the storm would come. The storm that would end the time out of time. He was healed now, and a warrior prince, so healed, could not abide monotony.

'It's enough,' she said calmly, 'because it's what we have.'

'For how much longer?' he demanded. 'Ten years? Fifty?'

'For as long as there is.'

Though she tried to pull away, he turned her hands over. 'You work them raw, haul buckets like a milkmaid.'

'Should I sit on my throne with soft white hands folded and let my people work?'

'There are other choices.'

'Not for me.'

'Come with me.' He gripped her arms now, tight, firm, as if he held his own life.

Oh, she'd dreamed of it, in her most secret heart. Riding off with him, flying through the forest and away to beyond. Toward the sun, the green, the flowers.

Into summer.

'I can't. You know I can't.'

'We'll find the way out. When we're home, I'll gather men, horses, provisions. I'll come back for your people. I swear it to you.'

'You'll find the way out.' She laid her hands on his chest, over the thunder of his heart. 'I believe it. If I didn't I would have you chained before I'd allow you to leave. I won't risk your death. But the way back ... ' She shook her head, turned away from him when his grip relaxed.

'You don't believe I'll come back.'

She closed her eyes because she didn't believe it, not fully. How could he turn his back on the sun and risk everything to travel here again for what he'd known for only a few weeks? 'Even if you tried, there's no certainty you'd find us again. Your coming was a miracle. Your safe passage home will be another. I don't ask for three in one lifetime.'

She drew herself up. 'I won't ask for your life, nor will I accept it. I will send a man with you – my best, my strongest – if you will take him. If you will give him good horses, and provisions, I will send others if the gods show him the way back again.'

'But you won't leave.'

'I'm bound to stay, as you are bound to go.' She turned back, and though tears stung her throat, her eyes were dry. 'It's said that if I leave here while winter holds this place, Rose Castle will vanish from sight, and all within will be trapped for eternity.'

'That's nonsense.'

'Can you say that?' She gestured to the white sky above the dome. 'Can you be sure of it? I am queen of this world, and I am prisoner.'

'Then bid me stay. You've only to ask it of me.'

'I won't. And you can't. First, you're destined to be king. It is your fate, and I have seen the crown you'll wear inside your own mind and heart. And more, your family would grieve and your people mourn. With that on your conscience, the gift we found together would be forever tainted. One day you would go in any case.'

'So little faith in me. I ask you this: Do you love me?'

Her eyes filled, sheened, but the tears did not fall. 'I care for you. You brought light inside me.'

'"Care" is a weak word. Do you love me?'

'My heart is frozen. I have no love to give.'

'That is the first lie you've told me. I've seen you cuddle a fretful babe in your arms, risk your life to save a small boy.'

'That is a different matter.'

'I've been inside you.' Frustrated fury ran over his face. 'I've seen your eyes as you opened to me.'

She began to tremble. 'Passion is not love. Surely my father had passion for my mother, for her sister. But love he had for neither. I care for you. I desire you. That is all I have to give. The gift of a heart, woman to man, has doomed me.'

'So because your father was feckless, your mother foolish, and your aunt vindictive, you close yourself off from the only true warmth there is?'

'I can't give what I don't have.'

'Then take this, Deirdre of the Sea of Ice. I love you, and I will never love another. I leave tomorrow. I ask you again, come with me.'

'I can't. I can't,' she repeated, taking his arm. 'I beg you. Our time is so short, let us not have this chill between us.

I've given you more than ever I gave a man. I pledge to you now there will never be another. Let it be enough.'

'It isn't enough. If you loved, you'd know that.' One hand gripped the hilt of his sword as if he would draw it and fight what stood between them. Instead, he stepped back from her. 'You make your own prison, my lady,' he said, and left her.

Alone, Deirdre nearly sank to her knees. But despair, she thought, would solve no more than Kylar's bright sword would. So she picked up the pail.

'Why didn't you tell him?'

Deirdre jolted, nearly splashing water over the rim. 'You have no right to listen to private words, Orna.'

Ignoring the stiff tone, Orna came forward to heft the bag of turnips. 'Hasn't he the right to know what may break the spell?'

'No.' She said it fiercely. 'His choices, his actions must be his own. He is entitled to that. He won't be influenced by a sense of honor, for his honor runs through him like his blood. I am no damsel who needs rescuing by a man.'

'You are a woman who is loved by one.'

'Men love many women.'

'By the blood, child! Will you let those who made you ruin you?'

'Should I give my heart, take his, at the risk of sacrificing all who depend on me?'

'It doesn't have to be that way. The curse—'

'I don't know love.' When she whirled around, her face was bright with temper. 'How can I trust what I don't know? She who bore me couldn't love me. He who made me never even looked on my face. I know duty, and I know the tenderness I feel for you and my people. I know joy and sadness. And I know fear.'

'It's fear that traps you.'

'Haven't I the right to fear?' Deirdre demanded. 'When I hold lives in my hands, day and night? I cannot leave here.'

'No, you cannot leave here.' The undeniable truth of that broke Orna's heart. 'But you can love.'

'And loving, risk trapping him in this place. This cold place. Harsh payment for what he's given me. No, he leaves on the morrow, and what will be will be.'

'And if you're with child?'

'I pray I am, for it is my duty.' Her shoulders slumped. 'I fear I am, for then I will have imprisoned his child, our child, here.' She pressed a hand to her stomach. 'I dreamed of a child, Orna, nursing at my breast and watching me with my lover's eyes, and what moved through me was so fierce and strong. The woman I am would ride away with him to save what grows inside me. The queen cannot. You will not speak of this to him, or anyone.'

'No, my lady.'

Deirdre nodded. 'Send Dilys to me, and see that provisions are set aside for two men. They will have a long and difficult journey. I await Dilys in the parlor.'

She set the bucket aside and walked quickly away.

Before going inside, Orna hurried through the archway and into the rose garden.

When she saw that the tiny leaf she'd watched unfurl from a single green bud was withering, she wept.

9

Even pride couldn't stop her from going to him. When time was so short there was no room for pride in her world. She brought him gifts she hoped he would accept.

And she brought him herself.

'Kylar.' She waited at his chamber door until he turned from the window where he stared out at the dark night. So handsome, she thought, her dark prince. 'Would you speak with me?'

'I'm trying to understand you.'

That alone, that he would try, lightened her heart. 'I wish you could.' She came forward and laid what she carried on the chest by his bed. 'I've brought you a cloak, since yours was ruined. It was my grandfather's, and with its lining of fur is warmer than what you had. It befits a prince. And this brooch that was his. Will you take it?'

He crossed to her, picked up the gold brooch with its carved rose. 'Why do you give it to me?'

'Because I treasure it.' She lifted a hand, closed it over his on the brooch. 'You think I don't cherish what you've given me, what you've been to me. I can't let you leave believing that. I can't bear the thought of you going when there's anger and hard words between us.'

There was a storm in his eyes as they met hers. 'I could take you from here, whether you're willing or not. No one could stop me.'

'I would not allow it, nor would my people.'

He stepped closer, and circled her throat with his hand with just enough force that the pulse against his palm fluttered with fear. 'No one could stop me.' His free hand clamped over hers before she could draw her dagger. 'Not even you.'

'I would never forgive you for it. Nor lie willingly with you again. Anger makes you think of using force as an answer. You know it's not.'

'How can you be so calm, and so sure, Deirdre?'

'I'm sure of nothing. And I am not calm. I want to go with you. I want to run and never look back, to live with you in the sunlight. To once smell the grass, to breathe the summer. Once,' she said in a fierce whisper. 'And what would that make me?'

'My wife.'

The hand under his trembled, then steadied before she drew it away. 'You honor me, but I will never marry.'

'Because of who made you, how you were made?' He took her by the shoulders now so that their gazes locked. 'Can you be so wise, so warm, Deirdre, and at the same time so cold and closed?'

'I will never marry because my most sacred trust is to do no harm. If I were to take a husband, he would be king. I would share the welfare of all my people with him. This is a heavy burden.'

'Do you think I would shirk it?'

'I don't, no. I've been inside your mind and heart. You keep your promises, Kylar, even if they harm you.'

'So you spurn me to save me?'

'Spurn you? I have lain with you. I have shared with you my body, my mind, as I have never shared with another. Will never share again in my lifetime. If I take your vow and keep you here, if you keep your vow and stay, how many will be harmed? What destinies would we alter if you did not take your place as king in your own land? And if I went with you, my people would lose hope. They would have no one to look to for guidance. No one to heal them. There is no one here to take my place.'

She thought of the child she knew grew inside her.

'I accept that you must go, and honor you for it,' she said. 'Why can't you accept that I must stay?'

'You see only black and white.'

'I *know* only black and white.' Her voice turned desperate now, with a pleading he'd never heard from her. 'My life, the whole of it, has been here. And one single purpose was taught to me. To keep my people alive and well. I've done this as best I can.'

'No one could have done better.'

'But it isn't finished. You want to understand me?' Now she moved to the window, pulled the hangings over the black glass to shut out the dark and the cold. 'When I was a babe, my mother gave me to Orna. I never remember my mother's arms around me. She was kind, but she couldn't love me. I have my father's eyes, and looking at me caused her pain. I felt that pain.'

She pressed her hands to her heart. 'I felt it inside me, the hurt and the longing and the despair. So I closed myself off from it. Hadn't I the right?'

There was no room for anger in him now. 'She had no right to turn from you.'

'She did turn from me, and that can't be changed. I was tended well, and taught. I had duties, and I had playmates. And once, when I was very young there were dogs. They died off, one by one. When the last ... his name was Griffen – a foolish name for a dog, I suppose. He was very old, and I couldn't heal him. When he died, it broke something in me. That's foolish, too, isn't it, to be shattered by the death of a dog.'

'No. You loved him.'

'Oh, I did.' She sat now, with a weary sigh. 'So much love I had for that old hound. And so much fury when I lost him. I was mad with grief and tried to destroy the ice rose. I thought if I could chop it down, hack it to bits, all this would end. Somehow it would end, for even death could never be so bleak. But a sword is nothing against magic. My mother sent for me. There would be loss, she told me. I had to accept it. I had duties, and the most vital was to care for my people. To put their well-being above my own. She was right.'

'As a queen,' Kylar agreed. 'But not as a mother.'

239

'How could she give what she didn't have? I realize now, with her bond with the animals, she must have felt grief as I did for the loss. She *was* grief, my mother. I watched her pine and yearn for the man who'd ruined her. Even as she died, she wept for him. His deceit, his selfishness stole the color and warmth from her life, and doomed her and her people to eternal winter. Yet she died loving him, and I vowed that nothing and no one would ever rule my heart. It is trapped inside me, as frozen as the rose in the tower of ice outside this window. If it were free, Kylar, I would give it to you.'

'You trap yourself. It's not a sword that will cut through the ice. It's love.'

'What I have is yours. I wish it could be more. If I were not queen, I would go with you on the morrow. I would trust you to take me to beyond, or would die fighting to get there with you. But I can't go, and you can't stay. Kylar, I saw your mother's face.'

'My mother?'

'In your mind, your heart, when I healed you. I would have given anything, anything, to have seen such love and pride for me in the eyes of the one who bore me. You can't let her grieve for a son who still lives.'

Guilt clawed at him. 'She would want me happy.'

'I believe she would. But if you stay, she will never know what became of you. Whatever you want for yourself, you have too much inside you for her to leave her not knowing. And too much honor to turn away from your duties to your family and your own land.'

His fists clenched. She had, with the skill of a soldier, out-flanked him. 'Does it always come to duty?'

'We're born what we're born, Kylar. Neither you nor I could live well or happy if we cast off our duty.'

'I would rather face a battle without sword or shield than leave you.'

'We've been given these weeks. If I ask you for one more night, will you turn me away?'

'No.' He reached for her hand. 'I won't turn you away.'

He loved her tenderly, then fiercely. And at last, when dawn trembled to life, he loved her desperately. When the night was over, she didn't cling, nor did she weep. A part of him wished she would do both. But the woman he loved was strong, and helped him prepare for his journey without tears.

'There are rations for two weeks.' She prayed it would be enough. 'Take whatever you need from the forest.' As he cinched the saddle on his horse, Deirdre slipped a hand under his cloak, laid it on his side.

And he moved away. 'No.' More than once during the night, she'd tried to explore his healing wound. 'If I have pain, it's mine. I won't have it be yours. Not again.'

'You're stubborn.'

'I bow before you, my lady. The queen of willful.'

She managed a smile and laid a hand on the arm of the man she'd chosen to guide the prince. 'Dilys. You are Prince Kylar's man now.'

He was young, tall as a tree and broad of shoulder. 'My lady, I am the queen's man.'

This time she touched his face. They had grown up together, and once had romped as children. 'Your queen asks that you pledge now your loyalty, your fealty, and your life to Prince Kylar.'

He knelt in the deep and crusted snow. 'If it is your wish, my queen, I so pledge.'

She drew a ring from her finger, pressed it into his hand. 'Live.' She bent to kiss both his cheeks. 'And if you cannot return—'

'My lady.'

'If you cannot,' she continued, lifting his head so their gazes met, 'know you have my blessing, and my wish for your happiness. Keep the prince safe,' she whispered. 'Do not leave him until he's safe. It is the last I will ever ask of you.'

She stepped back. 'Kylar, prince of Mrydon, we wish you safe journey.'

He took the hand she offered. 'Deirdre, queen of the Sea of Ice, my thanks for your hospitality, and my good wishes to you and your people.' But he didn't release her hand. Instead, he took a ring of his own and slid it onto her finger. 'I pledge to you my heart.'

'Kylar—'

'I pledge to you my life.' And before the people gathered in the courtyard, he pulled her into his arms and kissed her, long and deep. 'Ask me now, one thing. Anything.'

'I will ask you this. When you're safe again, when you find summer, pluck the first rose you see. And think of me. I will know, and be content.'

Even now, he thought, she would not ask him to come back for her. He touched a hand to the brooch pinned to his cloak. 'Every rose I see is you.' He vaulted onto his horse. 'I will come back.'

He spurred his horse toward the archway with Dilys trotting beside him. The crowd rushed after them, calling, cheering. Unable to resist, Deirdre climbed to the battlements, stood in the slow drift of snow and watched him ride away from her.

His mount's hooves rang on the ice, and his black cloak

snapped in the frigid wind. Then he whirled his horse, and reared high.

'I will come back!' he shouted.

When his voice echoed back to her, over her, she nearly believed it. She stood, her red cloak drawn tight, until he disappeared into the forest.

Alone, her legs trembling, she made her way down to the rose garden. There was a burning inside her chest, and an ache deep, deep within her belly. When her vision blurred, she stopped to catch her breath. With a kind of dull surprise she reached up to touch her cheeks and found them wet.

Tears, she thought. After so many years. The burning inside her chest became a throbbing. So. She closed her eyes and stumbled forward. So, the frozen chamber that trapped her heart could melt after all. And, melting, bring tears.

Bring a pain that was like what came with healing.

She collapsed at the foot of the great ice rose, buried her face in her hands.

'I love.' She sobbed now, rocking herself for comfort. 'I love him with all I am or will ever be. And it hurts. How cruel to show me this, to bring me this. How bitter your heart must have been to drape cold over what should be warmth. But you did not love. I know that now.'

Steadying as best she could, she turned her face up to the

dull sky. 'Even my mother did not love, for she willed him back with every breath. I love, and I wish the one who has my heart safe, and whole and warm. For I would not wish this barren life on him. I'll know when he feels the sun and plucks the rose. And I will be content.'

She laid a hand on her heart, on her belly. 'Your cold magic can't touch what's inside me now.'

And drawing herself up, turning away, she didn't see the delicate leaf struggling to live on a tiny green bud.

The world was wild, and the air itself roared like wolves. The storm sprang up like a demon, hurling ice and snow like frozen arrows. Night fell so fast that there was barely time to gather branches for fuel.

Wrapped in his cloak, Kylar brooded into the fire. The trees were thick here, tall as giants, dead as stones. They had gone beyond where Deirdre harvested trees and into what was called the Forgotten.

'When the storm passes, can you find your way back from here?' Kylar demanded. Though they sat close to warm each other, he was forced to shout to be heard over the screaming storm.

Dilys's eyes, all that showed beneath the cloak and hood, blinked once. 'Yes, my lord.'

'Then when travel is possible again, you'll go back to Rose Castle.'

'No, my lord.'

It took Kylar a moment. 'You will do as I bid. You have pledged your obedience to me.'

'My queen charged me to see you safe. It was the last she said to me. I will see you safe, my lord.'

'I'll travel more quickly without you.'

'I don't think this is so,' Dilys said in his slow and thoughtful way. 'I will see you home, my lord. You cannot go back to her until you have reached home. My lady needs you to come back to her.'

'She doesn't believe I will. Why do you?'

'Because you are meant to. You must sleep now. The road ahead is longer than the road behind.'

The storm raged for hours. It was still dark, still brutal when Kylar awoke. Snow covered him, turning his hair and cloak white, and even the fur did little to fight the canny cold.

He moved silently to his horse. It would take, he knew, minutes only to move far enough from camp that his trail would be lost. In such a hellish world, you could stand all but shoulder to shoulder with another and not see him beside you.

The man Dilys would have no choice but to return home when he woke and found himself alone.

But though he walked his horse soundlessly through the deep snow, he'd gone no more than fifty yards when Dilys was once more trudging beside him.

Brave of heart and loyal to the bone, Kylar thought. Deirdre had chosen her man well.

'You have ears like a bat,' Kylar said, resigned now.

Dilys grinned. 'I do.'

Kylar stopped, jumped down from the horse. 'Mount,' he ordered. 'If we're traveling through hell together, we'll take turns riding.' When Dilys only stood and stared, Kylar swore. 'Will you argue with me over everything or do as your lady commanded and I now bid?'

'I would not argue, my lord. But I don't know how to mount the horse.'

Kylar stood in the swirling snow, cold to the marrow of his bones, and laughed until he thought he would burst from it.

10

On the fourth day of the journey, the wind rose so fierce that they walked in blindness. Hoods, cloaks, even Cathmor's dark hide were white now. Snow coated Dilys's eyebrows and the stubble of his beard, making him look like an old man rather than a youth not yet twenty.

Color, Kylar thought, was a stranger to this terrible world. Warmth was only a dim memory in the Forgotten.

When Dilys rode, Kylar waded through snow that reached his waist. At times he wondered if it would soon simply bury them both.

Fatigue stole through him and with it a driving urge just to lie down, to sleep his way to a quiet death. But each time he stumbled, he pulled himself upright again.

He had given her a pledge, and he would keep it. She had willed him to live, through pain and through magic. So he would live. And he would go back to her.

Walking or riding, he slipped into dreams. In dreams he sat with Deirdre on a jeweled bench in a garden alive with roses, brilliant with sunlight.

Her hands were warm in his.

So they traveled a full week, step by painful step, through ice and wind, through cold and dark.

'Do you have a sweetheart, Dilys?'

'Sir?'

'A sweetheart?' Taking his turn in the saddle, Kylar rode on a tiring Cathmor with his chin on his chest. 'A girl you love.'

'I do. Her name is Wynne. She works in the kitchens. We'll wed when I return.'

Kylar smiled, drifted. The man never lost hope, he thought, nor wavered in his steady faith. 'I will give you a hundred gold coins as a marriage gift.'

'My thanks, my lord. What is gold coins?'

Kylar managed a weak chuckle. 'As useless just now as a

bull with teats. And what is a bull, you'd ask,' Kylar continued, anticipating his man. 'For surely you've seen a teat in your day.'

'I have, my lord, and a wonder of nature they are to a man. A bull I have heard of. It is a beast, is it not? I read a story once—' Dilys broke off, raising his head sharply at the sound overhead. With a shout, he snagged the horse's reins, dragged at them roughly. Cathmor screamed and stumbled. Only instinct and a spurt of will kept Kylar in the saddle as the great tree fell inches from Cathmor's rearing hooves.

'Ears like a bat,' Kylar said a second time while his heart thundered in his ears. The tree was fully six feet across, more than a hundred in length. One more step in its path and they would have been crushed.

'It is a sign.'

The shock roused Kylar enough to clear his mind. 'It is a dead tree broken by the weight of snow and ice.'

'It is a sign,' Dilys said stubbornly. 'Its branches point there.' He gestured, and still holding the reins, he began to lead the horse to the left.

'You would follow the branches of a dead tree?' Kylar shook his head, shrugged. 'Very well, then. How could it matter?'

He dozed and dreamed for an hour. Walked blind and stiff for another. But when they stopped for midday rations from their dwindling supply, Dilys held up a hand.

'What is that sound?'

'The bloody wind. Is it never silent?'

'No, my lord. Beneath the wind. Listen.' He closed his eyes. 'It is like . . . music.'

'I hear nothing, and certainly no music.'

'There.'

When Dilys went off at a stumbling run, Kylar shouted after him. Furious that the man would lose himself without food or horse, he mounted as quickly as he could manage and hurried after.

He found Dilys standing knee-deep in snow, one hand lifted, and trembling. 'What is it? My lord, what is this thing?'

'It's only a stream.' Concerned that the man's mind had snapped, Kylar leaped down from the horse. 'It's just a . . . a stream,' he whispered as the import raced through him. 'Running water. Not ice, but running water. The snow.' He turned a quick circle. 'It's not so deep here. And the air. Is it warmer?'

'It's beautiful.' Dilys was hypnotized by the clear water rushing and bubbling over rock. 'It sings.'

'Yes, by the blood, it is, and it does. Come. Quick now. We follow the stream.'

The wind still blew, but the snow was thinning. He could see clearly now, the shape of the trees, and tracks from game. He had only to find the strength to draw his bow, and they would have meat.

There was life here.

Rocks, stumps, brambles began to show themselves beneath the snow. The first call of a bird had Dilys falling to his knees in shock.

Snow had melted from their hair, their cloaks, but now it was Dilys's face that was white as ice.

'It's a magpie,' Kylar told him, both amused and touched when his stalwart man trembled at the sound. 'A song of summer. Rise now. We've left winter behind us.'

Soon Cathmor's hooves hit ground, solid and springy, and a single beam of light streamed through trees that were thick with leaves.

'What magic is this?'

'Sun.' Kylar closed his hand over the rose brooch. 'We found the sun.' He dismounted and on legs weak and weary walked slowly to a brilliant splash of color. Here, at the edge of the Forgotten, grew wild roses, red as blood.

He plucked one, breathed in its sweet scent, and said: 'Deirdre.'

And she, carrying a bucket of melted snow to her garden, swayed. She pressed a hand to her heart as it leaped with joy. 'He is home.'

She moved through her days now with an easy contentment. Her lover was safe, and the child they'd made warm inside her. The child would be loved, would be cherished. Her heart would never be cold again.

If there was yearning in her, it was natural. But she would rather yearn than have him trapped in her world.

On the night she knew he was safe, she gave a celebration with wine and music and dancing. The story would be told, she decreed, of Kylar of Mrydon. Kylar the brave. And of the faithful Dilys. And all of her people, all who came after, would know of it.

On a silver chain around her neck, she wore his ring.

She hummed as she cleared the paths in her rose garden.

'You sent men out to scout for Dilys,' Orna said.

'It is probably too early. But I know he'll start for home as soon as he's able.'

'And Prince Kylar. You don't look for him?'

'He doesn't belong here. He has family in his world, and

one day a throne. I found love with him, and it blooms in me – heart and womb. So I wish for him health and happiness. And one day, when these memories have faded from his mind, a woman who loves him as I do.'

Orna glanced toward the ice rose, but said nothing of it. 'Do you doubt his love for you?'

'No.' Her smile was warm and sweet as she said it. 'But I've learned, Orna. I believe he was sent to me to teach me what I never knew. Love can't come from cold. If it does, it's selfish, and is not love but simply desire. It gives me such joy to think of him in the sunlight. I don't wish for him as my mother wished for my father, or curse him as my aunt cursed us all. I no longer see my life here as prison or duty. Without it, I would never have known him.'

'You're wiser than those who made you.'

'I'm luckier,' Deirdre corrected, then leaned on her shovel as Phelan rushed into the garden.

'My lady, I've finished my story. Will you hear it?'

'I will. Fetch that shovel by the wall. You can tell me while we work.'

'It's a grand story.' He ran for the shovel and began heaving snow with great enthusiasm. 'The best I've done. And it begins like this: Once, a brave and handsome prince from a far-off land fought a great battle against men who would plunder his kingdom and kill his people. His name was Kylar, and his land was Mrydon.'

'It is a good beginning, Phelan the bard.'

'Yes, my lady. But it gets better. Kylar the brave defeated the invaders, but, sorely wounded, became lost in the great forest known as the Forgotten.'

Deirdre continued to work, smiling as the boy's words brought her memories back so clearly. She remembered her first glimpse of those bold blue eyes, that first foolish brush of lips.

She would give Phelan precious paper and ink to scribe the story. She would bind it herself in leather tanned from deer hide. In this way, she thought with pride, her love would live forever.

One day, their child would read the story, and know what a man his father was.

She cleared the path past jeweled benches, toward the great frozen rose while the boy told his tale and labored tirelessly beside her.

'And the beautiful queen gave him a rose carved on a brooch that he wore pinned over his heart. For days and nights, with his faithful horse, Cathmor, and the valiant and true Dilys, he fought the wild storms, crossed the iced shadows of the Forgotten. It was his lady's love that sustained him.'

'You have a romantic heart, young bard.'

'It is a *true* story, my lady. I saw it in my head.' He continued on, entertaining and delighting her with words of Dilys's stubborn loyalty, of black nights and white days, of a giant tree crashing and leading them toward a stream where water ran over rock like music.

'Sunlight struck the water and made it sparkle like diamonds.'

A bit surprised by the description, she glanced toward him. 'Do you think sun on water makes diamonds?'

'It makes tiny bright lights, my lady. It dazzles the eye.'

Something inside her heart trembled. 'Dazzles the eye,' she repeated on a whisper. 'Yes, I have heard of this.'

'And at the edge of the Forgotten grew wild roses, fire-red. The handsome prince plucked one, as he had promised, and when its sweetness surrounded him, he said his lady's name.'

'It's a lovely story.'

'It is not the end.' He all but danced with excitement.

'Tell me the rest, then.' She started to smile, to rest on her shovel. Then there came the sound of wild cheering and shouts from without the garden.

'This is the end!' The boy threw his shovel carelessly aside and raced to the archway. 'He is come!'

'Who?' she began, but couldn't hear her own voice over the shouts, over the pounding of her blood.

Suddenly the light went brilliant, searing into her eyes so that with a little cry of shock, she threw a hand up to shield them. Wild wind turned to breeze soft as silk. And she heard her name spoken.

Her hand trembled as she lowered it, and her eyes blinked against a light she'd never known. She saw him in the archway of the garden, surrounded by a kind of shimmering halo that gleamed like melted gold.

'Kylar.' Her heart, every chamber filled with joy, bounded in her breast. Her shovel clattered on the path as she ran to him.

He caught her up, spinning her in circles as she clung to him. 'Oh, my love, my heart. How can this be?' Her tears fell on his neck, her kisses on his face. 'You should not be here. You should never have come back. How can I let you go again?'

'Look at me. Sweetheart, look at me.' He tipped up her chin. 'So there are tears now. I'd hoped there would be. I ask you again. Do you love me, Deirdre?'

'So much I could live on nothing else my whole life. I

would not have had to risk yours to come back.' She laid her palms on his cheeks. Then her lips trembled open, her fingers shook. 'You came back,' she whispered.

'I would have crossed hell for you. Perhaps I did.'

She closed her eyes. 'That light. What is that light?'

'It is the sun. Unveiled. Here, take off your cloak. Feel the sun, Deirdre.'

'I'm not cold.'

'You'll never be cold again. Open your eyes, my love, and look. Winter is over.'

Gripping his hand, she turned to watch the snow melting away, vanishing before her staring eyes. Blackened stalks began to crackle, break out green and at their feet soft, tender blades of grass spread in a shimmering carpet.

'The sky.' Dazed, she reached up as if she could touch it. 'It's blue. Like your eyes. Feel it, feel the sun.' She held her hands out to cup the warmth.

On a cry of wonder, she knelt, ran her hands over the soft grass, brought her hands to her face to breathe in the scent. Though tears continued to fall, she laughed and held those hands out to him. 'Is it grass?'

'It is.'

'Oh.' She covered her face with her hands again, as if she could drink it. 'Such perfume.'

He knelt with her, and would remember, he knew, the rapture on her face the first time she touched a simple blade of grass. 'Your roses are blooming, my lady.'

Speechless, she watched buds spear, blooms unfold. Yellows, pinks, reds, whites in petals that flowed from bud to flower, and flowers so heavy they bent the graceful green branches. The fragrance all but made her drunk.

'Roses.' Her voice quivered as she reached out to touch, felt the silky texture. 'Flowers.' And buried her face in blooms.

She squealed like a girl when a butterfly fluttered by her face and landed on a tender bud to drink.

'Oh!' There was so much, almost too much, and she was dizzy from it. 'See how it moves! It's so beautiful.'

In turn, she tipped her face back and drank in the sunlight.

'What is that across the blue of the sky? That curve of colors?'

'It's a rainbow.' Watching her was like watching something be born. And once again, he thought, she humbled him. 'Your first rainbow, my love.'

'It's lovelier than in the books. In them it seemed false and impossible. But it's soft and it's real.'

'I brought you a gift.'

'You brought me summer,' she murmured.

'And this.' He snapped his fingers, and through the arch, down the path raced a fat brown puppy. Barking cheerfully, it leaped into Deirdre's lap. 'His name is Griffen.'

Drowned in emotion, she cradled the pup as she might a child, pressed her face into its warm fur. She felt its heartbeat, and the quick, wet lash of its tongue on her cheek.

'I'm sorry,' she managed, and broke down and sobbed.

'Weep, then.' Kylar bent to touch his lips to her hair. 'As long as it's for joy.'

'How can this be? How can you bring me so much? I turned you away, without love.'

'No, you let me go, with love. It took me time to understand that – and you. To understand what it cost you. There would have been no summer if I hadn't left you, and returned.'

He lifted her damp face now, and the puppy wiggled free and began to race joyfully through the garden. 'Is that not so?'

'It is so. Only the greatest and truest love, freely given, could break the spell and turn away winter.'

'I knew. When I plucked the rose, I understood. I watched summer bloom. It came with me through the forest. As I rode, the trees behind me went into leaf, brooks and streams sprang free of ice. With every mile I put behind me, every mile I came closer to you, the world awoke. Others will come tomorrow. I couldn't wait.'

'But how? How did you come back so quickly?'

'My land is only a day's journey from here. It was magic that kept you hidden. It's love that frees you.'

'It's more.' Phelan wiggled his way through the crowd of people who gathered in the archway. He gave a cry of delight as the pup leaped at him. 'It is truth,' he began, 'and sacrifice and honor. All these tied by love are stronger than a shield of ice and break the spell of the winter rose. When summer comes to Rose Castle, the Isle of Winter becomes the Isle of Flowers and the Sea of Ice becomes the Sea of Hope. And here, the good queen gives hand and heart to her valiant prince.'

'It is a good ending,' Kylar commented. 'But perhaps you would wait until I ask the good queen for her hand and her heart.'

She dashed tears from her cheeks. Her people, her love, would not see her weep at such a time. 'You have my heart already.'

'Then give me your hand. Be my wife.'

She put her hand in his, but because she must be a queen, turned first to her people. 'You are witness. I pledge myself in love and in marriage, for a lifetime, to Kylar, prince of Mrydon. He will be your king, and to him you will give your service, your respect, and your loyalty. From this day, his people will be your brothers and your sisters. In time, our lands will be one land.'

She let them cheer, let his name ring out along with hers into the wondrous blue bowl of sky. And her hand was warm in Kylar's.

'Prepare a feast of celebration and thanks, and make ourselves ready to welcome the guests that come on the morrow. Leave us now, for I need a moment with my betrothed. Take the pup to the kitchen, Phelan, and see that he is well fed. Keep him for me.'

'Yes, my lady.'

'His name is Griffen.' Her gaze met Orna's, and smiled as her people left her alone with her prince. 'There is one last thing to be done.'

She walked with him down the path to where the reddest roses bloomed on the tallest bush under thinning ice. Without a thought, she plunged her hand through it, and the shield shattered like glass. She picked the first rose of her life, offered it to him.

'I've accepted you as queen. That is duty. Now I give myself to you as a woman. This is for love. You brought light to my world. You freed my heart. Now and forever, that heart is yours.'

She started to kneel, and he stopped her. 'You won't kneel to me.'

Her brows lifted, and command once again cloaked her. 'I am queen of this place. I do as I wish.' She knelt. 'I am yours, queen and woman. From this hour, this day will be known and celebrated as Prince Kylar's Return.'

With a gleam in his eye, he knelt as well, and made her lips twitch. 'You will be a willful wife.'

'This is truth.'

'I would not have it otherwise. Kiss me, Deirdre the fair.'

She put a hand on his chest. 'First, I have a gift for you.'

'It can wait. I lived on dreams of your kisses for days in the cold.'

'This gift can't wait. Kylar, I have your child in me. A child made from love and warmth.'

The hand that had touched her face slid bonelessly to her shoulder. 'A child?'

'We've made life between us. A miracle, beyond magic.'

'Our child.' His palm spread over her belly, rested there as his lips took hers.

'It pleases you?'

For an answer he leaped up, hoisted her high until her laughter rang out. She threw her arms toward the sky, toward the sun, the sky, the rainbow.

And the roses grew and bloomed until branches and flowers reached over the garden wall, tumbled down, and filled the air with the promise of summer.

IF YOU ENJOYED THESE STORIES
KEEP READING FOR A SPECIAL PREVIEW
OF

THE WITNESS

AVAILABALE NOW FROM PIATKUS

June 2000

Elizabeth Fitch's short-lived teenage rebellion began with L'Oréal Pure Black, a pair of scissors and a fake ID. It ended in blood.

For nearly the whole of her sixteen years, eight months and twenty-one days she'd dutifully followed her mother's directives. Dr. Susan L. Fitch issued *directives,* not orders. Elizabeth had adhered to the schedules her mother created, ate the meals designed by her mother's nutritionist and prepared by her mother's cook, wore the clothes selected by her mother's personal shopper.

Dr. Susan L. Fitch dressed conservatively, as suited—in her opinion— her position as chief of surgery of Chicago's Silva Memorial Hospital. She expected, and directed, her daughter to do the same.

Elizabeth studied diligently, accepting and excelling in the academic programs her mother outlined. In the fall, she'd return to Harvard in pursuit of her medical degree. So she could become a doctor, like her mother—a surgeon, like her mother.

Elizabeth—never Liz or Lizzie or Beth—spoke fluent Spanish, French, Italian, passable Russian and rudimentary Japanese. She played both piano and violin. She'd traveled to Europe, to Africa. She could name all the bones, nerves and muscles in the human body and play Chopin's Piano Concerto—both Nos. 1 and 2, by rote.

She'd never been on a date or kissed a boy. She'd never roamed the mall with a pack of girls, attended a slumber party or giggled with friends over pizza or hot fudge sundaes.

She was, at sixteen years, eight months and twenty-one days, a product of her mother's meticulous and detailed agenda.

That was about to change.

She watched her mother pack. Susan, her rich brown hair

already coiled in her signature French twist, neatly hung another suit in the organized garment bag, then checked off the printout with each day of the week's medical conference broken into subgroups. The printout included a spreadsheet listing every event, appointment, meeting and meal, scheduled with the selected outfit, with shoes, bag and accessories.

Designer suits; Italian shoes, of course, Elizabeth thought. One must wear good cuts, good cloth. But not one rich or bright color among the blacks, grays, taupes. She wondered how her mother could be so beautiful and deliberately wear the dull.

After two accelerated semesters of college, Elizabeth thought she'd begun—maybe—to develop her own fashion sense. She had, in fact, bought jeans *and* a hoodie *and* some chunky-heeled boots in Cambridge.

With cash, so the receipt wouldn't show up on her credit card bill, in case her mother or their accountant checked and questioned the items, which were currently hidden in her room.

She'd felt like a different person wearing them, so different she'd walked straight into a McDonald's and ordered her first Big Mac with large fries and a chocolate shake.

The pleasure had been so huge, she'd had to go into the bathroom, close herself in a stall and cry a little.

The seeds of the rebellion had been planted that day, she supposed, or maybe they'd always been there, dormant, and the fat and salt had awakened them.

But she could feel them, actually feel them, sprouting in her belly now.

"Your plans changed, Mother. It doesn't follow that mine have to change with them."

Susan took a moment to precisely place a shoe bag in the Pullman, tucking it just so with her beautiful and clever surgeon's hands, the nails perfectly manicured. A French manicure, as always—no color there, either.

"Elizabeth." Her voice was as polished and calm as her wardrobe. "It took considerable effort to reschedule and have you admitted to the summer program this term. You'll complete the requirements for your admission into Harvard Medical School a full semester ahead of schedule."

Even the thought made Elizabeth's stomach hurt. "I was promised a three-week break, including this next week in New York."

"And sometimes promises must be broken. If I hadn't had this coming week off, I couldn't fill in for Dr. Dusecki at the conference."

"You could have said no."

"That would have been selfish and shortsighted." Susan

brushed at the jacket she'd hung, stepped back to check her list. "You're certainly mature enough to understand the demands of work overtake pleasure and leisure."

"If I'm mature enough to understand that, why aren't I mature enough to make my own decisions? I want this break. I need it."

Susan barely spared her daughter a glance. "A girl of your age, physical condition and mental acumen hardly *needs* a break from her studies and activities. In addition, Mrs. Laine has already left for her two-week cruise, and I could hardly ask her to postpone her vacation. There's no one to fix your meals or tend to the house."

"I can fix my own meals and tend the house."

"Elizabeth." The tone managed to merge clipped with long-suffering. It's settled."

"And I have no say in it? What about developing my independence, being responsible?"

"Independence comes in degrees, as does responsibility and freedom choice. You still require guidance and direction. Now, I've e-mailed you an updated schedule for the coming week, and your packet with the information on the program is on your desk. Be sure to thank Dr. Frisco personally for making room for you in the summer term."

As she spoke, Susan closed the garment bag, then her

small Pullman. He stepped to her bureau to check her hair, her lipstick.

"You don't listen to anything I say."

In the mirror, Susan's gaze shifted to her daughter. The first time, Elizabeth thought, her mother had bothered to actually look at her since she'd come into the bedroom. "Of course I do. I heard everything u said, very clearly."

"Listening's different than hearing."

"That may be true, Elizabeth, but we've already had this discussion."

"It's not a discussion, it's a decree."

Susan's mouth tightened briefly, the only sign of annoyance. When she turned, her eyes were coolly, calmly blue. "I'm sorry you feel that way. As your mother, I must do what I believe best for you."

"What's best for me, in your opinion, is for me to do, be, say, think, act, want, become exactly what you decided for me before you inseminated yourself with precisely selected sperm."

She heard the rise of her own voice but couldn't control it, felt the hot sting of tears in her eyes but couldn't stop them. "I'm tired of being your experiment. I'm tired of having every minute of every day organized, orchestrated and choreographed to meet your expectations. I want to make my own choices, buy my own clothes, read books *I* want to read. I want to live my own life instead of yours."

Susan's eyebrows lifted in an expression of mild interest. "Well. Your attitude isn't surprising, given your age, but you've picked a very inconvenient time to be defiant and argumentative."

"Sorry. It wasn't on the schedule."

"Sarcasm's also typical, but it's unbecoming." Susan opened her briefcase, checked the contents. "We'll talk about all this when I get back. I'll make an appointment with Dr. Bristoe."

"I don't need therapy! I need a mother who *listens,* who gives a shit about how I feel."

"That kind of language only shows a lack of maturity and intellect."

Enraged, Elizabeth threw up her hands, spun in circles. If she couldn't be calm and rational like her mother, she'd be *wild.* "Shit! Shit! Shit!"

"And repetition hardly enhances. You have the rest of the weekend to consider your behavior. Your meals are in the refrigerator or freezer, and labeled. Your pack list is on your desk. Report to Ms. Vee at the university at eight on Monday morning. Your participation in this program will ensure your place in HMS next fall. Now, take my garment bag downstairs, please. My car will be here any minute."

Oh, those seeds were sprouting, cracking that fallow ground and pushing painfully through. For the first time in her life, Elizabeth looked straight into her mother's eyes and said, "No."

She spun around, stomped away and slammed the door of her bedroom. She threw herself down on the bed, stared at the ceiling with tear-blurred eyes. And waited.

Any second, any second, she told herself. Her mother would come in, demand an apology, demand obedience. And Elizabeth wouldn't give one, either.

They'd have a fight, an actual fight, with threats of punishment and consequences. Maybe they'd yell at each other. Maybe if they yelled, her mother would finally hear her.

And maybe, if they yelled, she could say all the things that had crept up inside her this past year. Things she thought now had been inside her forever.

She didn't want to be a doctor. She didn't want to spend every waking hour on a schedule or hide a stupid pair of jeans because they didn't fit her mother's dress code.

She wanted to have friends, not approved socialization appointments. She wanted to listen to the music girls her age listened to. She wanted to know what they whispered about and laughed about and talked about while she was shut out.

She didn't want to be a genius or a prodigy.

She wanted to be normal. She just wanted to be like everyone else.

She swiped at the tears, curled up, stared at the door.

Any second, she thought again. Any second now. Her mother had to be angry. She had to come in and assert authority. Had to.

"Please," Elizabeth murmured as seconds ticked into minutes. "Don't make me give in again. Please, please, don't make me give up."

Love me enough. Just this once.

But as the minutes dragged on, Elizabeth pushed herself off the bed. Patience, she knew, was her mother's greatest weapon. That, and the unyielding sense of being right, crushed all foes. And certainly her daughter was no match for it.

Defeated, she walked out of her room, toward her mother's.

The garment bag, the briefcase, the small, wheeled Pullman were gone. Even as she walked downstairs, she knew her mother had gone, too.

"She left me. She just left."

Alone, she looked around the pretty, tidy living room. Everything perfect—the fabrics, the colors, the art, the arrangement. The antiques passed down through generations of Fitches—all quiet elegance.

Empty.

Nothing had changed, she realized. And nothing would.

"So I will."

She didn't allow herself to think, to question or second-guess. Instead, she marched back up, snagged scissors from her study area.

In her bathroom, she studied her face in the mirror—coloring she'd gotten through paternity—auburn hair, thick like her mother's but without the soft, pretty wave. Her mother's high, sharp cheekbones, her biological father's—whoever he was—deep-set green eyes, pale skin, wide mouth.

Physically attractive, she thought, because that was DNA and her mother would tolerate no less. But not beautiful, not striking like Susan, no. And that, she supposed, had been a disappointment even her mother couldn't fix.

"Freak." Elizabeth pressed a hand to the mirror, hating what she saw in the glass. "You're a freak. But as of now, you're not a coward."

Taking a big breath, she yanked up a hunk of her shoulder-length hair and whacked it off.

With every snap of the scissors she felt empowered. *Her* hair, *her* choice. She let the shorn hanks fall on the floor. As she snipped and hacked, an image formed in her mind. Eyes narrowed, head angled, she slowed the clipping. It was just geometry, really, she decided—and physics. Action and reaction.

The weight—physical and metaphorical, she thought—just fell away. And the girl in the glass looked lighter. Her eyes seemed bigger, her face not so thin, not so drawn.

She looked . . . new, Elizabeth decided.

Carefully, she set the scissors down, and, realizing her breath was heaving in and out, made a conscious effort to slow it.

So short. Testing, she lifted a hand to her exposed neck, ears, then brushed them over the bangs she'd cut. Too even, she decided. She hunted up manicure scissors, tried her hand at styling.

Not bad. Not really good, she admitted, but different. That was the whole point. She looked, and felt, different.

But not finished.

Leaving the hair where it lay on the floor, she went into her bedroom, changed into her secret cache of clothes. She needed product—that's what the girls called it. Hair product. And makeup. And more clothes.

She needed the mall.

Riding on the thrill, she went into her mother's home office, took the spare car keys. And her heart hammered with excitement as she hurried to the garage. She got behind the wheel, shut her eyes a moment. "Here we go," she said quietly, then hit the garage-door opener and backed out.

She got her ears pierced. It seemed a bold if mildly painful move, and suited the hair dye she'd taken from the shelf after a long, careful study and debate. She bought hair wax, as she'd seen one of the girls at college use it and thought she could duplicate the look. More or less.

She bought two hundred dollars' worth of makeup because she wasn't sure what was right.

Then she had to sit down because her knees shook. But she wasn't done, Elizabeth reminded herself, as she watched the packs of teenagers, groups of women, teams of families, wander by. She just needed to regroup.

She needed clothes, but she didn't have a plan, a list, an agenda. Impulse buying was exhilarating, and exhausting. The temper that had driven her this far left her with a dull headache, and her earlobes throbbed a little.

The logical, sensible thing to do was go home, lie down for a while. Then plan, make that list of items to be purchased.

But that was the old Elizabeth. This one was just going to catch her breath.

The problem facing her now was that she wasn't precisely sure which store or stores she should go to. There were so many of them, and all the windows full of *things*. So she'd wander, watch for girls her age. She'd go where they went.

She gathered her bags, pushed to her feet—and bumped into someone.

"Excuse me," she began, then recognized the girl. "Oh. Julie."

"Yeah." The blonde with the sleek, perfect hair and melted-chocolate eyes gave Elizabeth a puzzled look. "Do I know you?"

"Probably not. We went to school together. I was student teacher in your Spanish class. Elizabeth Fitch."

"Elizabeth, sure. The brain trust." Julie narrowed her sulky eyes. "You look different."

"Oh. I . . ." Embarrassed now, Elizabeth lifted a hand to her hair. "I cut my hair."

"Cool. I thought you moved away or something."

"I went to college. I'm home for the summer."

"Oh, yeah, you graduated early. Weird."

"I suppose it is. Will you go to college this fall?"

"I'm supposed to go to Brown."

"That's a wonderful school."

"Okay. Well . . ."

"Are you shopping?"

"Broke." Julie shrugged—and Elizabeth took a survey of her outfit— the snug jeans, riding very low on the hip-bones, the skinny, midriff-baring shirt, the oversized shoulder bag and wedge sandals. "I just came to the mall to see my boyfriend—my *ex*-boyfriend, since I broke up with him."

"I'm sorry."

"Screw him. He works at the Gap. We were supposed to go out tonight, and now he says he has to work till ten, then wants to hang out with his bros after. I've had it, so I dumped him."

Elizabeth started to point out that he shouldn't be penalized for honoring his obligations, but Julie kept talking—and it occurred to Elizabeth that the other girl hadn't spoken more than a dozen words to her since they'd known each other.

"So I'm going over to Tiffany's, see if she wants to hang, because now I've got no boyfriend for the summer. It sucks. I guess you hang out with college guys." Julie gave her a considering look. "Go to frat parties, keggers, all that."

"I . . . There are a lot of men at Harvard."

"Harvard." Julie rolled her eyes. "Any of them in Chicago for the summer?"

"I couldn't say."

"A college guy, that's what I need. Who wants some loser who works at the mall? I need somebody who knows how to have fun, who can take me places, buy alcohol. Good luck with that, unless you can get into the clubs. That's where they hang out. Just need to score some fake ID."

"I can do that." The instant the words were out, Elizabeth wondered where they'd come from. But Julie gripped her arm, smiled at her as if they were friends.

"No bull?"

"No. That is, it's not very difficult to create false identi-fication with the right tools. A template, photo, laminate, a computer with Photo-shop."

"Brain trust. What'll it take for you to make me a driver's license that'll get me into a club?"

"As I said, a template—"

"No, Jesus. What do you want for it?"

"I . . ." Bargaining, Elizabeth realized. A barter. "I need to buy some clothes, but I don't know what I should buy. I need someone to help me."

"A shopping buddy?"

"Yes. Someone who knows. You know."

Eyes no longer sulky, voice no longer bored, Julie simply beamed. "That's *my* brain trust. And if I help you pick out some outfits, you'll make me up the ID?"

"Yes. And I'd also want to go with you to the club. So I'd need the right clothes for that, too."

"You? Clubbing? More than your hair's changed, Liz."

Liz. She was Liz. "I'd need a photo, and it will take a little while to construct the IDs. I could have them done tomorrow. What club would we go to?"

"Might as well go for the hottest club in town. Warehouse 12. Brad Pitt went there when he was in town."

"Do you know him?"

"I wish. Okay, let's go shopping."

It made her dizzy, not just the way Julie piloted her into a store, snatched up clothes with only the most cursory study. But the *idea* of it all. A shopping buddy. Not someone who preselected what was deemed appropriate and expected her to assent. Someone who grabbed at random and talked about looking hot, or cool, even sexy.

No one had ever suggested to Elizabeth that she might look sexy.